"We are not friends, no point in engaging *You do not care abou.* my childhood, *nor I yours.*

You care about what I am doing to your precious company, and I care about returning the Chatsfield name to its former glory. We are not on opposite sides, no matter how you wish to view it. And we don't need to engage in polite banter in order to pretend we like each other."

Her eyes had narrowed considerably. And her color was high. The flush over her breasts was intriguing. Christos wanted to slip her gown off her shoulder and press his mouth just above her heart.

"With an attitude like that, no wonder you don't have any friends. You refuse to let anyone get close enough to be a friend."

He snorted. "And do you really want to be my friend, Lucilla? Or is there something more to this query?"

She tilted her chin up. "No, I don't want to be your friend. But I *was* trying to be polite. I thought maybe life would be easier if we at least pretended to like one another."

He took a step closer to her, watched the thrum of her pulse kick up in her neck. He had to admire that she did not back away. She stood her ground, though she had to tilt her head back to look up at him since he towered over her.

"I am quite willing to pretend, Lucilla *mou*. I find myself utterly intrigued by the cut of that gown and the mystery of what lies beneath. If you wish, we can leave together and pretend to like each other in my bed."

Heiress's Defiance

Lynn Raye Harris

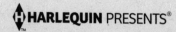

Special thanks and acknowledgment are given to Lynn Raye Harris for her contribution to The Chatsfield series.

Recycling programs
for this product may
not exist in your area.

ISBN-13: 978-0-373-13295-9

Heiress's Defiance

First North American Publication 2014

Copyright © 2014 by Harlequin Books S.A.

HARLEQUIN®
www.Harlequin.com

Printed in U.S.A.

All about the author...
Lynn Raye Harris

USA TODAY bestselling author **LYNN RAYE HARRIS**
burst onto the scene when she won a writing contest
held by Harlequin®. The prize was an editor for a
year—but only six months later, Lynn sold her first
novel. A former finalist for the Romance Writers
of America's Golden Heart Award, Lynn lives in
Alabama with her handsome husband and two crazy
cats. Her stories have been called "exceptional and
emotional," "intense," and "sizzling." You can visit her
at www.lynnrayeharris.com.

Other titles by Lynn Raye Harris available in ebook:

Thanks to all my readers for always being there.
Hope you enjoy my first Greek hero!
And thanks to Donna Braswell, who helped me
with Greek words and culture, and who invited me
to the Philoptochos tea. Any mistakes are
my fault and not the lovely Donna's. Enjoy!

CHAPTER ONE

"Take care of it now," Christos Giatrakos said into the phone, his voice hard and clipped and way sexier than Lucilla would have liked. Oh, how she hated Christos! And yet, sitting here in his office, waiting for him to finish whatever dictatorial phone call he was currently making, her belly churned with heat at the mere sound of that voice.

Certainly it did not help that he looked more like a male underwear model than a CEO. Christos should have been strutting his stuff on a runway in Milan, dressed in nothing but his tightie-whities, instead of sitting in what should be *her* chair—at what should be *her* desk—and making everyone's lives miserable.

Especially her life. She'd worked too damn hard and too damn long, and sacrificed too damn much, to have this Greek god of an upstart usurping her position in her own family company.

Lucilla ran a hand over her sleek twist, making sure her hair wasn't out of place, and fumed. She wanted to get up and walk out, but she couldn't let Christos see that he had that much power to anger her. He'd summoned her by email, as he so often did, and then forced her to cool her heels on his couch while he made phone calls.

She sat ramrod straight, with her tablet on her lap, scrolled through emails and pretended not to care that Christos was ignoring her. Her gaze took in the office that should have been hers. Christos hadn't claimed the desk in the manner that she'd expected, but there were subtle differences—the way the computer sat at a precise angle, the pen—worth more than her monthly salary—perfectly positioned in line with the keyboard, and a small coin sitting just to the right of the pen. From where she was sitting she could only tell that the coin wasn't English. The photographs that had once lined her father's desk had been pushed back into the corner of the bookcase behind the desk. Her mother's ancient edition of *Aesop's Fables* was still in its usual position in the case, however.

"If you can't get this done, then don't call back. The Chatsfield has other suppliers, Ron. And I will not hesitate to use them."

Christos put the phone back in the cradle with a firm click and muttered something in Greek. And then he looked up, hitting her with the full force of those icy blue eyes. Lucilla shrugged off the internal shiver making its way down her spine and met his gaze evenly.

"What is the problem with the Frost wedding reception this weekend?"

Lucilla's insides boiled at his tone. No polite greeting, no reasonable query. Just a demand. And an insulting one at that.

"Problem? There is no problem, Christos." She refused to call him Mr. Giatrakos, though he insisted on it from all the employees. Well, damn him, she wasn't just any employee. She was the rightful CEO of this company and she refused to act subservient just because her father had chosen this man over her. Not happening.

His gaze did not soften. "I have heard there is a problem."

At times like this, Lucilla wanted to wrap her hands around his gorgeous neck and squeeze. "Then you heard wrong." She flipped through the schedule on her tablet and ran down the page of tasks for the Frosts. "The only thing that could have ever been considered a minor issue—and trust me, it is not an issue for us—is the seating arrangements for the bride's mother and father. I have taken care of it."

"And why would this have been an issue?"

"Because they are divorcing, acrimoniously as it happens, and Mr. Frost is attending with his new, much younger girlfriend. Something he should know better than to do but apparently does not."

Christos's eyes were chips of ice. "Lucca may have pulled off the coup of the century and made a success of the royal wedding in Preitalle, but this means now, more than ever, the world's eye is upon us. And the Frosts' wedding has the potential to explode in our faces, Lucilla. You will see that it does not."

Lucilla stood and tried not to look flustered. Dammit. Every time he said her name, a heated shudder rolled through her. His accent wasn't heavy, but it was definitely pronounced, and the way it rolled over the syllables of her name was too sensual, too disturbing. Yet he would not call her Ms. Chatsfield because she would not call him Mr. Giatrakos. In that respect, it was her own fault. If she didn't like her name on his lips, she had no one to blame but herself.

"I have been seeing that things do not explode for

quite some time. I will continue to do so, even when you are history."

And he would be history, if she had anything to say about it. If Antonio came through with the hostile take-over of the Kennedy Group, they could prove to their father that they did not need Christos Giatrakos. How-ever, given that Antonio had missed their meeting last week she was starting to worry.

Lucilla frowned. The only thing that bothered her about the scheme was Antonio himself. Although An-tonio was living in this hotel, she wasn't seeing him any more than she had over the past few years. And when she'd seen him this last time he'd looked…differ-ent somehow. More agitated and preoccupied.

Concern speared into her at the thought of her big brother, but she pushed it aside and concentrated on the man before her. If they could just get rid of Christos, life could be good again. They would all be happier when she and Antonio were in control of the family empire once more.

And that was a goal she intended to work tirelessly for.

One corner of Christos's mouth lifted in a grin. It was not a friendly grin, however, and she cursed herself for showing her irritation yet again. Sometimes, she just could not help her reaction.

"I am not history at the moment, Lucilla *mou,* and you will do as you are told or face the consequences."

Lucilla tried so hard to keep her tongue in check. But some things were impossible to stomach. "You have no control over me, Christos, no matter what you think. Yes, you control the Chatsfield empire, and you con-trol access to my trust fund. But you won't intimidate me the way you've intimidated my family." She walked over and put her palms on his desk, leaned over until her eyes were at the same level as his. She was all in now, her emotions whipped to a furious froth that had been bubbling for weeks, ever since this man showed up and started giving orders like a despot.

"I won't be bullied by the likes of you. You need me right here, doing what it is I do every day, or you *will* fail. I've been running this hotel for years. Fire me, and see what happens then. My father will send you packing without a shred of remorse once you fail to do whatever it is he thinks you're going to do."

Christos's eyes glittered. He stood, very slowly, and Lucilla straightened. Even in her heels, she wasn't as tall as he was. He looked down on her as if she were a bug beneath his custom shoe.

"You've been wanting to say that for a while, have you not?" His voice was mild, amused, and yet it also managed to be hard and unflinching.

Her heart raced, her skin heating from the inside out. Yes, she'd been holding it in, and yes, it felt good to finally say what she'd been thinking. But she also felt as if she'd committed an error. She'd admitted to the enemy that she cared very much about his elevation over her when what she really needed to do was be quiet and take him down from the inside.

She absolutely could not let him get wind of what she'd talked Antonio into doing.

Because she *would* take this arrogant Greek down. One way or the other, Christos Giatrakos's reign would be short and sweet, a footnote in the history of the hotel chain. It still stung that her father had chosen this stranger over her, but she could not let her wounded feelings get in the way of what she had to do to win.

Yes, she should have kept her mouth shut. But she hadn't, and now there was nothing to do but own it. Lucilla tilted her chin up. "I have indeed. You might be congratulating yourself on dispersing my siblings on your errands, but don't think you'll handle me quite so easily."

His eyes slid over her then, and her stomach clenched. "I wouldn't dream of *handling* you, Lucilla. But if I did, rest assured you would do as I wished. And you would enjoy every moment of it."

Her heart lodged in her throat. Were they still talking about the hotel? Or about something else?

"You are a deluded man, Christos. I will never enjoy a moment with you. I despise you and wish you would crawl back into whatever hole you crawled out of."

His expression changed then, went from coolly amused and arrogant to hard and cold and…resentful? Lucilla blinked. She had the impression she'd hurt him, but that could not be possible. Christos Giatrakos had no heart to wound.

His next words proved it. "I care not what you think of me, Lucilla *mou*. You are as spoiled and useless as the rest of your kind." He held up a hand to stop any protests. "Oh, you play at working, and you do a good enough job in your duties as the director of guest services. You are correct that I need you, but make no mistake—if I have to fire you, I will. No one is indispensable to the running of this company, Lucilla. Not even you."

"Or you," she threw back at him.

One eyebrow lifted. "Or me. And that is as it should be. Any company that is so invested in the talents of a single person and cannot recover should that person die or leave is a very stupid company indeed. My goal is to make the Chatsfield number one in the luxury field again. But I do not expect that this company will not ever run without me, nor would I want it to. That, I believe, is the difference between us. You would see it fail out of spite. I would see it succeed."

There was a pinch in her chest as she pulled in a sharp breath. Of all the arrogant assumptions. Yes, she wanted the Chatsfield to be number one again—but she didn't think it took Christos to do it. She could have done it if her father had given her the chance. She still could. She *would.*

"I do not wish to see us fail at all. And I resent that you would think so."

"Then grow up and act like it." He flicked his hand. "And now if you will get out of my office, I have important work to do."

Lucilla clutched her tablet tight to stop her from flinging it at his head. "As you command, O Lord of Everything." She took two steps, then whirled back around to find him still watching her. "You won't always be here, Christos. Enjoy the big corner office while you can."

He lowered himself into the plush leather chair with a smile. Then the arrogant bastard had the nerve to lean back and put his feet on the ancient cherry desk.

"I am enjoying it very much, thank you. Now be a good girl and get to work."

Lucilla stalked out of his office with her head held high. But she could feel the blood pounding in her veins, feel the hate coursing through her. She wanted to scream. And, perversely, she wanted to kiss the bastard. She marched past Jessie—her able assistant—and into her own, much smaller office, slamming the door satisfyingly before throwing herself into her chair and closing her eyes while she fought for calm.

Why on earth could she not face the damn man without thinking about how his lips must taste? It was getting worse, not better. Every time she was with him, she thought of how he might taste, of how those muscles would feel beneath her hands. It was just her perverse nature, going left when she wanted to go right. She'd always been this way. Tell her she couldn't do something and she set out to prove she could.

Like run the hotel chain. She'd spent years proving she was the rightful heir to the CEO position, and what did her father do? He hired a smoldering Greek with a bad attitude and a sexier-than-sin body to do the job she'd been training for all her life. She'd put her dreams aside at the age of fourteen, when her mother had walked out and left her and Antonio, her older brother, to be the surrogate parents for their siblings. Her father had been useless after Liliana left and so it had fallen to her and Antonio.

Well, dammit, she'd done what she was supposed to do. She'd been a good girl and played by rules that should never have been imposed on her at such a young age. She'd done her time and she wanted her due. She wanted control of the Chatsfield empire. The hotels were in her blood. They were not in Christos's. He was not a Chatsfield and he didn't care, other than where dollars, pounds and euros were concerned.

Lucilla chewed her lip, thinking. She'd researched Christos thoroughly when he'd arrived, but there was one thing she couldn't find out. He didn't seem to come from anywhere. He didn't have a family. He was Greek, he claimed Athens as his hometown, and that was it.

There'd been no record of his life before he was about twenty-five and burst onto the scene as the man who'd turned around a very old and venerable shipping company.

Then he'd moved on to another company, and another. He was good at what he did—and ruthless beyond belief. He slashed and burned and what emerged from the ashes was always better and brighter than before.

Yes, he was pretty good. But she didn't trust him. And she damn sure didn't like him. She couldn't believe that her father had turned over control to this man they knew so little about. Gene Chatsfield had handed over the keys to the kingdom and then flown back to the U.S. to be with his new fiancée as if he hadn't just turned Lucilla's world—and her siblings' worlds—upside down in the process.

Lucilla wanted to know more. She wanted to know who Christos Giatrakos really was, where he came from and why he thought he could be so cold and ruthless with everyone. And then she wanted him gone.

That, really, was the deciding factor. Lucilla wanted him *gone,* no matter how sexy or smoldering he was. And she was willing to do just about anything to achieve that goal. She picked up the phone. It was time to call in every last favor she was owed in exchange for information.

The Chatsfield was hosting a gala tonight in the main ballroom. An art auction for charity that would bring out the richest members of London society. As CEO, it was Christos's duty to be there as the new public face of the company. Whatever the Chatsfield children had done to tarnish the venerable name, Christos was determined to erase those memories from the public consciousness. Yes, it would take time, but he would turn the company around. Of that he had no doubt.

He frowned as he thought of Lucilla Chatsfield standing in his office and glaring at him. She didn't like him; that much was plain. He didn't like her, either. She was utterly spoiled, though perhaps not quite as useless as most of her siblings.

Yet he found her oddly compelling and he did not like it. For instance, her brown eyes were flecked with gold. Why did he know this detail? He had no idea, but he did. And whenever she came into his office, he found himself watching those gold flecks and wondering if they might change with passion. What would staid Lucilla look like mussed? Her hair was always sleek and smooth, either twisted up on her head or slicked back into a thick ponytail. Her suits were crisp and tailored. Not too conservative, not too sexy.

He should not notice her at all, really. She was not a classically beautiful woman. Her cheeks were a little too plump and her hips a little too curvy to be stylish. She was too serious and frowned entirely too much.

And yet he found himself wondering what she would look like naked and sprawled across his bed. A clear sign he'd been working too much and not getting enough sex if he was thinking of uptight Lucilla Chatsfield this way.

Tonight, that would change. He had a date to the gala, and she'd hinted more than once that she was available all night long. After a trip home to shower and change into his tuxedo, Christos got behind the wheel of his Bugatti Veyron and went to pick Victoria up at her apartment. She was waiting just inside the glass doors, her blond hair a mass of luscious curls, her body encased in something shiny that looked almost like rubber.

She sashayed from the building and two men on the sidewalk nearly tripped on their tongues. Christos should be ecstatic at the sight of her, and yet he was somehow disappointed as he opened the door and helped her into the car. *She is lovely,* he told himself. *Lovely.*

"I've been looking forward to tonight," Victoria said, sliding her hand up his thigh once he'd gotten into the driver's seat again. She leaned in and kissed him on the cheek. Other than the shock of being touched so blatantly, he felt no excitement. His body responded as her hand drifted over him—a woman was touching his groin, after all—but he didn't find the prospect particularly thrilling.

"Enough of that, Victoria," he clipped out. "We have a long evening to get through first."

She laughed and ran her thumb over his cheek, presumably removing the lipstick she'd left there. "I can't wait, darling."

Soon, they were at the hotel, and Christos went around to join Victoria on the red carpet while the valet slipped inside his car and drove off. Photographers were stationed on either side of the entrance, corralled behind velvet ropes, their flashes popping again and again as he walked up the carpet with Victoria on his arm.

They passed inside. Staff members were busily taking care of the guests, but he had no doubt he'd been seen. No one nodded, though. He did not expect it. It wasn't his job to be liked. Gene Chatsfield had hired him because he was the best. Not because he was the nicest.

The gala was in full swing when they walked into the ballroom. The soaring art-deco walls and ceilings were a work of art themselves, which is why the room showcased the art on display so well. Men in tuxedos and women in glittering gowns mingled, drinks in hand, rotating past the displays and making marks in their catalogs.

Christos circulated, shaking hands and talking with the guests, smiling with satisfaction at their compliments on the decor and service. Victoria clung to his side until he grew tired of having her there and deposited her with a group of expensively dressed women. When he left, they were comparing notes on their dress designers.

He continued to talk to the guests as the clock ticked down to the moment the auction was scheduled to start. At one point, when the conversation bored him and his mind began to drift, the crowd parted and a flash of red caught his eye. It was a dark-haired woman, standing with her back to him, her body encased in a clinging ruby gown sewn with sparkling crystals. She was alone in front of a painting, and he had a sudden urge to find out just what she seemed so captivated by that others did not.

He did not know her or what drove her, but she appeared lonely and isolated in the single beam of light shining down on the spot she stood in. Her head was bowed, her shoulders bent forward, as if the weight of something terribly sad pressed down on her.

Her isolation and loneliness spoke to him because he so often felt the same things. By choice, yes, but still. He'd had to isolate himself to survive the hell of his childhood. It was a skill he'd perfected by the time he was fourteen. A necessary skill to keep from going insane in the juvenile-detention facility he'd been sent to.

Christos excused himself from the conversation and

moved toward the woman. He wanted to know who she was and what was in the picture that affected her so much. She turned then, and he stopped, stunned. Lucilla Chatsfield's brows were pulled together, her face creased with sadness and pain. And she was utterly beautiful standing alone in that beam of light.

The light picked out her bone structure, highlighted the luminous quality of her skin and transformed the darkness of her hair into a chestnut cloud flowing down her back. She was still Lucilla, but Lucilla as he'd never seen her before. The beauty of her hit him like a lightning bolt, stole the air from his lungs, sent blood rushing into his groin.

He wanted to possess her. He wanted to erase that sadness from her eyes, and he wanted to strip that red dress from her body and expose the creamy skin underneath. The need to do so rocked him. And angered him.

He had no time for this. Lucilla was an obstacle in his path, not a dalliance on the side. She hated him. Despised him for sending her brothers and sister away on errands, and for thwarting her ambition.

Christos plucked two glasses of champagne from a passing tray and moved toward her. She'd turned to look at the painting again, and he found himself focusing on the swell of her hips, the curve of her back and the lush beauty of her hair as it tumbled over her shoulders in rich, reddish-brown waves. She never wore her hair down. He was suddenly thankful that she did not because the urge to plunge his fingers into it and feel the silky mass gliding over his hand was almost overwhelming.

"See something you want?"

She whirled to face him, clutching a hand over her heart. "Oh, my God, you scared me."

He held out the champagne. "Then I apologize."

She took the glass. Then she turned to look at the painting again. "Isn't she beautiful?"

Christos stared at the small portrait of a woman. It wasn't an old painting, though it wasn't recent, either. The woman was wearing a long gown, pearls and a mink, and she was laughing. It was not a staid portrait at all. Christos frowned as he scanned the portrait. This woman looked familiar in a way. He turned to look at Lucilla's profile, saw the same lines as in the painting, and a new feeling took root in his soul: anger and even a modicum of pity. Gene Chatsfield had put a portrait of his missing ex-wife into the auction, and Lucilla seemed sad about it.

No one knew where Liliana Chatsfield had gone, but one day she'd walked out on her family and never came home again. He knew the history, as so many did, but for the first time he could see how it must have affected at least one Chatsfield child.

It made him feel almost tender toward her. A complication he did not need. "She is indeed. Your mother, I presume?"

She took a sip of her champagne and he saw that her fingers trembled. "Yes."

"And does it bother you this picture is in the auction?"

She sniffed. She did not look at him. "Of course not. It's for a good cause, and my father is right to get rid of it. Graham Laurent painted it before he was quite so famous, so it will fetch a high price simply because of that. Obviously, my father knows this."

And Gene Chatsfield was marrying again, so his new

wife-to-be probably didn't want a portrait of the old wife still in his possession. Though why he didn't gift it to one of his children, Christos couldn't say. It seemed the logical thing to do.

"You could buy it."

She turned to look up at him again, and he felt the power of that gaze down to his toes. The gold flecks in her eyes sparkled in the light from above. "Oh, no, I couldn't. It wouldn't be seemly."

He didn't quite understand that logic, but it was not his concern really. If she didn't want to buy it, what did he care?

"As you wish, Lucilla *mou*." He didn't know why he called her *my Lucilla,* but the first time he'd done it, she'd seemed annoyed—so he'd kept doing so because it amused him to irritate her. He had not meant to irritate her now, but of course she could not know that. Her eyes narrowed.

"Don't you have some souls to collect elsewhere in the room?"

Christos couldn't help the laugh that burst from him then. Lucilla tried to frown but ended up smiling, though she kept biting her lip to stop. He wished she would let it out because he was certain a smile would transform her face.

"I have met my quota of souls for the day, unfortunately."

She arched an eyebrow. "Tomorrow is a new day. I'm sure you'll find some lives to wreck before the morning runs out."

He took a sip of champagne, uncharacteristically amused. She was acerbic and tart, not at all what he was accustomed to in a woman. It was a novelty, and he enjoyed it more than he should. He never cared if he was liked. Companies hired him to do the tough jobs, to make the decisions no one else would.

He didn't care if this woman liked him, either—but he found himself hoping she wouldn't go away just yet.

"It is on my schedule," he said.

"Of course it is." She pulled in a deep breath and turned away from the painting as if she had made a final decision to slice herself off from the allure of it. "Tell me about you, Christos. Where did you grow up? What did you like to do as a child?"

Her questions punched him in the gut. He never talked about his childhood. It was too painful. Too dark and disgusting. Compared to hers, even with an absent mother, his was hell on earth.

"I grew up in Greece. I had a happy life, I got an education and I went to work. What else is there to know?" The lies flowed easily from his tongue these days. He'd had years to practice them, after all.

She was staring at him. "Where in Greece? Near the sea? Inland?"

Ice formed in his veins. He did not like it when people pried. "Everywhere in Greece is near the sea."

"That's a very vague answer."

He shrugged as if it were nothing to him. "We are not friends, Lucilla. There is no point in engaging in idle chitchat. You do not care about my childhood, nor I yours. You care about what I am doing to your precious company, and I care about returning the Chatsfield name and all it stands for to its former glory. We are not on opposite sides, no matter how you wish to view it. And we don't need to engage in polite banter in order to pretend we like each other."

Her eyes had narrowed considerably. And her color was high. The flush over her breasts was intriguing. He wanted to slip her gown off her shoulder and press his mouth just above her heart.

"With an attitude like that, no wonder you don't have any friends. You refuse to let anyone get close enough to be a friend."

He snorted. "And do you really want to be my friend, Lucilla? Or is there something more to this query?"

She tilted her chin up. "No, I don't want to be your friend. But I *was* trying to be polite. I thought maybe life would be easier if we at least pretended to like each other."

He took a step closer to her, watched the thrum of her pulse kick up in her neck. He had to admire that she did not back away. She stood her ground, though she had to tilt her head back to look up at him since he towered over her.

"I am quite willing to pretend, Lucilla *mou*. I find myself utterly intrigued by the cut of that gown and the mystery of what lies beneath. If you wish, we can leave together and pretend to like each other in my bed."

Her eyes grew as wide as saucers. The color in her cheeks bloomed redder than before. And then she looked completely furious, as if he'd tricked her somehow. He didn't have time to figure it out because she poked him in the chest with a manicured finger.

"You are not serious, Christos, and this isn't funny."

"I was not trying to be funny."

She poked him again, harder this time. "I saw you come in and I know who you're with. Don't insult me by pretending you find me more appealing than you do your supermodel girlfriend." She dropped her finger and straightened her shoulders. "I am not that desperate or that stupid and I resent you thinking I am."

CHAPTER TWO

LUCILLA'S HEART BEAT hard and fast as she met Christos's icy blue gaze. She knew her color was high, and she knew the hue of her gown didn't help matters in the least. Why had she chosen red for tonight?

Because she knew he would be here.

No, that was not it at all.

She'd chosen the sexiest, boldest dress she owned because she liked to look and feel pretty, not because Christos Giatrakos would be here with yet another model on his arm. Since he'd arrived at the Chatsfield, he'd often been seen at their various events with beautiful women—a different one every time, in fact.

And now he was making fun of her. Taunting her with the idea of them being together, of tangled limbs and heated skin, when she knew it was the furthest thing from his mind. It was his aim to fluster her. It infuriated her that she could even be flustered—damn her stupid hormones—but she refused to let him know it was working.

She tilted her chin up and gave him her best glare. It had often worked on her siblings when they were growing up and she needed to get them in line.

Christos smirked. And then his gaze slid from hers, down over her neck, her collarbone, her chest…

Her skin burned everywhere he looked, as if it were his hands gliding over her body rather than his eyes. "I assure you I am most serious, Lucilla *mou*. If you care to test me, take my hand and follow me."

She curled her free hand into a fist to prevent her from doing just that. Not that she seriously wanted to get naked with Christos, but she was damn tempted to call his bluff. Because he was baiting her. He wasn't serious, and they both knew it. And she would love nothing more than to make him admit it.

"Is this your famous seduction technique? I find it lacking in subtlety and quite amateurish indeed."

His gaze glittered. "You prove my point with your refusal. You are a coward, Lucilla. This is why you cannot run the Chatsfield Hotels. You are not willing to take chances."

A fresh wave of anger buffeted her. "Goading me will not get you anywhere. I can see through you, Christos. You want to prod me into doing something stupid. It would give you no greater pleasure than to make me look like an idiot."

"You do that quite well on your own."

She nearly choked on her own tongue. "How dare you."

He arched an eyebrow, mocking her. "I dare because you will not. Because you are frightened, Lucilla. A spoiled little girl who cannot make the hard choices in life. I can, and I will, best you every time."

"I hate you," she whispered, her heart hammering hard.

"I am aware of this. And I am certain it can only make this flame between us burn hotter."

"There is no flame. You're deluded." And yet her body was being eaten alive by excitement and anger and the very powerful urge to kiss this man, to see if she would incinerate with that single touch.

How had this...this *weakness* happened? One minute she was staring at her mother's portrait and the next he was there and she was burning up inside. She told herself it was because she'd been feeling sad and vulnerable and she hadn't yet gotten her defenses back up. That was the only way Christos could get to her like this.

He took a step closer to her, until there was hardly a breath separating them. "It is time to stop lying to yourself. You feel it the same as I do. You have felt it from the first moment, the same as I have. Let us burn together, Lucilla, and get this inconvenient attraction out of the way. We'll work together much better once it's done."

She couldn't breathe. He was taking up all the air, all the space, and she ached with his nearness. It was the final straw for her. She took a step backward, out of his orbit, and sucked in a deep breath. "I'm sorry, Christos, but I think you've got it all wrong. There is no attraction, at least not on my part. I can't stand you and I certainly don't want you. Now if you will excuse me, I have an event to supervise."

"You can tell yourself that, but we both know it's not true."

"You don't know anything about me," she said tightly.

"Run away, Lucilla. But this isn't over."

She sucked in an angry breath. "I am certain it is. Good night, Christos."

Lucilla pivoted on her heel and strode away, merging

into the crowd. She was shaking inside, and that infuriated her. Why did she let him get to her? For weeks now,
she'd been cool and businesslike, ignoring him, looking
down her nose at him even though he was taller than
she. She'd treated him like the bug under the dark rock
that he was, and she'd gotten away with it.

But today she'd lost her cool. She'd finally snapped
and all the boiling emotions she'd been trying so hard
to hide had spilled over the walls of the dam she'd built
to contain them. They were currently ravaging everything in their path despite her best attempts to rein them
in again.

But she *would* get herself under control. She had a
plan, and that plan required her to keep doing as she always did. Christos would be gone before the summer
was out when she was finished. She just had to stay
strong and focused.

Lucilla slipped into the ladies' room where she
smoothed her long hair and refreshed her lipstick. She
stepped back and studied herself in the mirror on one
wall. She was not unattractive. But she wasn't tall or
leggy, or so thin she could wear anything and look fabulous in it. She had curves and little bulges—thank heavens for proper foundation garments—and her cheeks
were too plump. She was also short, though four-inch
heels made her seem tall.

She had brown eyes and brown hair and her smile was
too wide. She did, however, have fabulous breasts. She
slipped her hands under their curves, admiring them in
the mirror. Yes, men definitely wanted these. Perhaps
Christos did, too, though it seemed far more likely he
was simply toying with her. Wanting her to admit she

wanted him so he could reject her and thus prove his superiority while laughing at her.

Not happening.

With a last primp of her hair, she returned to the ballroom. As the evening wore on, she smiled and chatted with the guests and tried to push Christos from her mind. It wasn't easy since she could feel his presence in the room. She knew he was watching and waiting and perhaps hoping she would make a mistake tonight.

She glimpsed him from time to time, holding court at the center of a gathering, the tall, leggy blonde in the skintight dress plastered to his side. He caught her gaze once and she forced herself not to look away. They stared at each other for several moments before the woman at his side seemed to realize his attention wasn't on her anymore. She leaned in close and said something in his ear, and then he was turning his perfect smile on her.

Lucilla felt almost bereft when he wasn't looking at her anymore, as if he'd somehow rejected her when he'd turned away. Utterly ridiculous.

She hadn't brought a date tonight. She hadn't dated anyone in months now because she'd been so focused on the hotel empire and had no time, but she decided that first thing tomorrow, she was getting back out there in the dating pool. It was ridiculous to throw herself so hard into work that she neglected having a personal life.

She told herself that if she hadn't been lonely and aching for companionship, Christos would not have been able to affect her.

And he *had* affected her. She would admit that much. He was tall, sinfully sexy, and he made her blood hum. She really hated that about herself, that she could be attracted to a jerk like him, but her body didn't seem to know he was poison.

When the auction began, Lucilla stayed around at first to make sure things were going smoothly, but then she retreated to her office with instructions to Jessie to come and get her if anything was amiss. She didn't want to be there for the auctioning of her mother's portrait.

She didn't know why it bothered her—Liliana Chatsfield had thought nothing of abandoning her children and husband and leaving the raising of her family to her two eldest, so why on earth should Lucilla care about her portrait?

It was nostalgia, plain and simple, and she refused to let it bother her a moment longer. She sat at her desk—not the easiest thing to do in a tight gown—and scrolled through the bookings and reports for the upcoming week. The hotel had many things going on, and it was her duty to make sure it all went smoothly.

When her door opened, she glanced up, expecting to see Jessie. Instead, her stomach dropped into her toes and her pulse kicked up at the sight of Christos standing there, coolly handsome in his tuxedo and crisp white shirt.

"Yes?" she said as blandly as possible.

He walked in and closed the door and her heart ticked up another notch. "You left rather abruptly. Is everything all right?"

"Why wouldn't it be?"

"You tell me."

She sighed and pushed her hair back over her shoulder. "It's been a long day, Christos. I'm tired and I have a lot of work to do. I don't stay for every event. Jessie knows where to find me if I'm needed."

"You are upset with me."

She rolled her eyes. "Not everything is about you, difficult as that may be to believe. No, I don't like you, but I don't spend every waking moment thinking about you." Well, she did, but much of it was about how to get rid of him. She waved a hand airily. "I forgot about it as soon as I started talking to the auction director."

Not quite true, but he didn't need to know that.

He sprawled in the chair in front of her desk, gloriously loose-limbed and casual when she had the impression he was anything but. "This is good, Lucilla *mou*. Because we have things to talk about."

She tried not to let the way he said her name slip down her spine and start drumming a beat in her deepest core, but it was damn near impossible. Plague the man for making her think of sex, anyway!

"I wish you wouldn't call me that. I have no idea what it means, but it irritates me."

His grin was too sexy for comfort. "I know this. It's why I do it. And it means '*my* Lucilla.'"

Her stomach clenched. "I am most certainly *not* your Lucilla. I'm not anyone's Lucilla."

She could have bitten her tongue for admitting that last part. It was as if she'd just come out and said she couldn't interest a man to save her life.

"This is a shame. You *should* be someone's Lucilla. You should be taken to bed often and made to scream your lover's name many times a night."

Her throat was tight. "You really shouldn't talk to me like this. It's inappropriate."

He ran his fingers along the edge of the chair's arm. "Is it? You have informed me more than once that you don't work for me, that you are a Chatsfield and these hotels are yours by birthright. How am I being inappropriate?"

She gritted her teeth and tried to ignore the pulsing of her blood in her veins. "My father hired you and gave you control over the Chatsfield Family Trust. I'd say that's incentive enough for me to need to do what you say. And that makes this conversation inappropriate."

"And here I thought we were finally being truthful with each other." He made it sound as if he was disappointed in her, and that only irritated her further.

"What did you wish to talk to me about, Christos? If it's not business, then please go away."

He laughed. "It is definitely business, Lucilla *mou*. But I cannot help but rib you now that I know you are not immune to my charm."

"Oh, for God's sake—you *have* no charm! This is not about you or your nonexistent charm. It's about business and what's best for the hotels, so stop irritating me and get on with it."

He leaned forward then and put his elbows on her desk. "After the shareholders' meeting in August, I plan to make a tour of several Chatsfield locations. You will accompany me."

Lucilla blinked. "Me? Why? Don't you have an assistant for that?"

He rubbed a finger over his bottom lip and she found herself following the motion of that finger. "If you wish to run this company someday, I suggest you do what I tell you."

She felt herself growling. "Sometimes it's easier to get flies with honey, you know." She tapped a key on her computer, purposely ignoring him. "And maybe I've decided I don't want the company, after all. Maybe I'll start my own business."

"You can try. Or you can come with me and help fix what is wrong."

She blinked. His tone hadn't changed at all, but he was now looking at her expectantly. As if he just knew what her answer would be. And, damn him, he did. But she wasn't going to make it easy on him.

"You cannot possibly mean for me to really help you. I'm spoiled and useless, remember?"

"You are indeed. And yet I am pleased with tonight's event, and pleased with how things have gone in your office in general. It's time to step up, Lucilla. Prove your mettle or get out of my way."

She gripped the pen she'd picked up just a little tighter. He was so damn smug. "I can handle anything you throw at me, baby."

He blinked. "Baby?"

"Annoying, right?" She shrugged, though her heart raced with adrenaline. "I've decided to start giving as good as I get. If I'm your Lucilla, you can be my baby."

He lifted an eyebrow, and she had the impression she'd just wakened a sleeping tiger. Perhaps she shouldn't bait him, but God, he deserved it. It made her feel reckless, which was certainly not how she usually behaved. But she rather liked it.

"I look forward to the inevitable clash of wills, Lucilla. You have no idea how much."

She dropped the pen. "Because you like discord in your work environment? Well, I don't. But I won't be bullied, either. So get ready, baby, because I will not back down."

He stood then and looked down at her from a great

height. Because she didn't like him towering over her, she stood, too. They faced each other across her desk. Her body felt rubbery, liquid, as their gazes held. There was no denying that Christos Giatrakos was powerfully, sinfully attractive.

If only he wasn't such an arrogant jerk.

"I feel as if we must seal this deal somehow," he murmured, and her stomach fluttered.

She came around her desk and thrust her hand out. She would not cower from him like a mouse. "I believe a handshake is how it's usually done."

His gaze dropped to her outstretched hand. "Indeed." His hand slipped into hers, engulfing it. They were palm to palm and it somehow felt like the most intimate touch imaginable. She tried not to gasp, tried not to shiver or make any response that let him know how intense this feeling was.

But she didn't need to. He tugged her hand softly and she moved forward until their bodies pressed together. His arm slipped behind her, his fingers spreading over the small of her back, burning her through the fabric of her dress.

His other hand tilted her chin up. His eyes, those beautiful, icy eyes, searched hers. She could not, for the life of her, imagine what she was supposed to say.

"I think this requires something a bit more personal," he murmured. And then his mouth came down on hers— softly, sweetly, his lips gliding over hers, teasing and tantalizing. Her heart was a reckless runaway in her chest, and her body had lost the ability to hold itself upright moments ago.

She clutched his lapels, her eyes fluttering closed as he tormented her with that glorious mouth. His tongue slipped over her lips, and she gasped. Then he was inside and she was there to meet him. Their tongues tangled, and Lucilla made a noise in her throat as her body simply melted.

Oh, she hadn't felt like this in so long—if ever. She'd had lovers, certainly. But not for months now, and no one who'd made her yearn so keenly for his touch. Kissing Christos was a revelation in more ways than one.

First, he was an amazing kisser. Second, in spite of her very real dislike of him, it only seemed to make kissing him more exciting. He tilted her chin up, plundered her mouth with a bit more urgency than before. His tongue was skillful, his lips masterful.

Oh, how she ached for more than this melding of mouths.

But this was Christos. *Christos.* The man her father had sent to do the job she was meant to do. The man who thought himself above her in every way. The man who showed absolutely no remorse or pity in his dealings with others.

He'd sent Lucca to the Mediterranean, Cara to Vegas, Franco on an errand in Australia. He'd hired Antonio as the head of strategy, but Antonio had taken the job only because she'd begged him to so they could work together to bring Christos down. With Orsino out of action in France, and Nicolo currently holed up at Chatsfield House with Christos's PA—whom he'd sent to secure Nicolo's attendance at the next shareholders' meeting—Christos was like a great spider, sitting at the center of his web and sending out threads designed to ensnare people.

Lucilla's fingers tightened in his lapels. She had a choice. She could stop this insanity or she could use this moment between them. She had never been a seductress before—but she could be. She could use this fire, this need, and she could best him at his own game.

She pressed herself closer to him, though it terrified her on some level to do so. His grip on her tightened, his hands spanning her hips, pulling her against him and—

Oh, my.

He was hard. There was no mistaking it. She'd thought, on some level, that he was faking desire for her. Liquid heat flooded her sex as he moved against her, his body sparking delicious sensations in hers. She let her hands slide over his chest, beneath his jacket—

There was a knock on the door and then it swung open before Lucilla registered what such an intrusion would mean.

"Oh! Excuse me!"

The door slammed shut again and Lucilla broke free of Christos's grip. Oh, my God. Her cheeks blazed. She'd just been caught in the arms of the boss. By Jessie. Because that's how everyone viewed Christos around here even if she did not.

Fury and embarrassment boiled in her belly. She'd been so convinced she knew what she was doing. What on earth had possessed her?

She was not a seductress and she had no idea what she'd do with Christos if she did sleep with him. How would that help her cause? Clearly, she'd been out of her mind. The moment he'd kissed her, she'd lost her sense. And now Jessie knew. Who else would know before the week was out?

Christos's eyes glittered hot as he ran a thumb over his lip, presumably removing her lipstick. He appeared as cool as if he were standing outside in a soaking rain while she felt as if she would never be cool again.

"It seems as if we've been interrupted. Not a moment too soon, I imagine."

"Honestly, I have no idea what that means." She went around her desk and stood with that object between them, as if it could protect her when she apparently didn't have sense enough to protect herself. "Nothing was going to happen."

"Don't lie to yourself." His voice was soft as a whisper and yet steely, too. "We wanted the same thing, Lucilla. And it would have happened on your desk in another five minutes."

"You are so deluded. I let you kiss me. It meant nothing."

"Tell yourself that if it helps you sleep at night. But you know as well as I do where that kiss was headed."

She folded her arms over her chest and hoped the wild beat of her pulse didn't show in her throat. "If you will excuse me, I believe Jessie needs to see me for something."

He inclined his head. "Of course." He was almost to the door when he turned and threw her a heated look. "As I said before, this is not over. In fact, I would say it has only begun."

Without waiting for a reply, he yanked the door open and stalked through it. An astonished and red-faced Jessie hurried into the room, eyes wide. She wisely did not say a word about Christos.

Lucilla took her seat and tried to appear cool. "Well, has there been a disaster?" Aside from the disaster of letting Christos kiss her and steal all her good sense, of course.

"Nothing of the sort. You asked me to let you know who bought your mother's portrait."

She'd almost forgotten. "Yes, of course I did."

Jessie looked apologetic. "I'm afraid it was an anonymous phone bidder. It sold for one hundred thousand pounds, though."

Lucilla tried to ignore the pinch in her heart. No way could she have afforded that much, even if she had been willing to bid. "Thank you, Jessie. I'll be here for a while. Let me know if I'm needed."

"Yes, Ms. Chatsfield," Jessie said before turning and hurrying out the door. Lucilla closed her eyes and leaned back in her chair. She could still feel Christos's touch on her skin, still feel the deep pull of desire in her core.

Lucilla shivered. And then she opened up her email and got to work. Christos had to go. Soon.

CHAPTER THREE

CHRISTOS WAS IN a bad mood. He was restless and edgy and his patience had run out a long time ago. He knew what it was. He sat at his desk in his big corner office and brooded over the latest reports. Oh, the reports were fine. There was progress on all fronts. Lucca wasn't making a spectacle of himself, Cara was managing to ride out the media storm created in Las Vegas with the notorious Aiden Kelly and Franco was getting somewhere with Purman Wines.

Not only that, but Sophie had made progress with Nicolo and he would be at the shareholders' meeting next week. Orsino still wasn't answering Christos's calls, but Christos figured it was only a matter of time. The Chatsfield children were coming into line, whether they believed it or not.

His biggest problem, however, was Lucilla.

He couldn't forget that kiss in her office on the night of the charity auction. It had been two weeks ago now and he thought of it incessantly. The way she'd melted in his arms like molten gold, her body curving into his and promising him such sweetness. He'd wanted her quite desperately in that moment. And she had wanted him, too; he was certain of it. She'd been ready to come apart in his arms and then the door had opened and Jessie had stumbled in—and that was the end of that.

For two weeks, she'd avoided him. They saw each other at the morning staff meetings. She gave her reports. But she did not come to his office—and he did not send for her.

He did it as much to prove to himself as to her that he was unaffected by their interchange. Yes, she'd excited him and he'd wanted her. But he did not need her. Women were interchangeable to him. All he required from them was a warm body in his bed and a few hours of passion. Beyond that, he wished for nothing more.

Needed nothing more.

Except, dammit, he couldn't stop thinking about Lucilla's mouth beneath his, her tongue gliding against his, her body so pliable and warm....

The tingle at the base of his spine was not a good sign. He swore and got to his feet, shoving his hands in his trouser pockets and stalking over to the window to gaze out on the park across the street. He needed a woman. Any woman. That would take the edge off and then he could get back to thinking straight again.

He could call Victoria. She was an enthusiastic lover, even if she left him cold. Yes, he'd taken her back to her apartment that night after the aborted kiss with Lucilla and he'd let her strip him naked. He'd spent his passion inside her body, but he'd felt vaguely disgusted with himself when it was done. Then he'd left her with a kiss and a promise to call.

He had not done so, of course. He had no intention of doing so, no matter that it would be the solution to his problem.

He raked a hand through his hair and swore softly. He

could not figure out this reaction to Lucilla, except that she fired his blood because she so very clearly despised him. He didn't usually care how anyone felt about him so long as the job got done. He still didn't care.

But he was intrigued, damn him. No one stood up to him the way Lucilla did. No one challenged him on every level. He found that he enjoyed it.

He was a man who got what he wanted. And right now, he wanted Lucilla Chatsfield. He wanted her beneath him, saying his name in pleasure rather than derision. It was dangerous to want such a thing, and yet he was driven by a need that went all the way back to his miserable childhood.

He'd been nobody, nothing, an unwanted blot on the dirty face of the life he came from. He'd clawed his way up, out of the mire, and he'd sworn he would have everything he had ever been denied. He'd not been raised with gold and diamonds and plenty to eat. He'd had to fight to survive, and he'd had to maim to prevent being killed.

Lucilla Chatsfield, in contrast, had grown up in a huge pile of stones known as Chatsfield House, where she'd had servants, money, all the food she could eat and the finest education money could buy. Her tones were cultured, her manner graceful and understated.

Lucilla would never be gauche. She would never be an urchin from a hardscrabble background. She would never feel as if she didn't belong.

He knew what it meant to be all those things, though he'd left them far behind. He'd achieved fame in certain circles, a fortune and all the women he wanted. He'd had heiresses before. Rich divorcées. Women whose pedigrees went back to some important monarch or other.

But there was something about Lucilla Chatsfield.

Something about the idea of seeing her naked and trembling before him, begging for his touch, for his mouth on her body. Begging the former street urchin to caress her privileged flesh.

Oh, yes, she made him remember his roots and he did not like it. She made him feel unworthy, and he'd worked a long time to banish that feeling. He'd not felt worthless in forever. Not until Lucilla looked down her nose at him and told him to crawl back in his hole.

What he didn't understand was *why* she made him feel that way, because she certainly wasn't the first to say such a thing to him. She likely wouldn't be the last.

But she did, and he couldn't allow it. Christos let out a long breath. There was only one cure, only one way to relegate her to her rightful place in his universe.

Lucilla was standing in the kitchen, tasting the selections the head chef suggested for the upcoming seasonal menu when Christos walked in. Her heart skipped a beat, but she continued to lift the tasting spoon to her lips and nibble on the goat-cheese-and-truffle-oil hors d'oeuvres Henri had designed. It was perfectly placed on a little crostini that gave it a delightful crunch when she bit down.

"Excellent, chef," she said after she'd swallowed the morsel.

"Sir?" Henri inquired, turning to Christos with a tasting spoon.

"Certainly." He took the spoon and popped the food into his mouth and she found herself fascinated with the way he chewed it. Slowly, as if savoring every flavor. When he finally swallowed, she wanted to fan herself. "Most excellent," he told the chef, who beamed.

Henri excused himself after a few more moments discussing the food and Lucilla found herself alone with Christos—or as alone as one could be in a kitchen bustling with activity. She hadn't spent any time with him since that night over two weeks ago when she'd nearly lost all her sense over nothing more than an illicit kiss.

Frustratingly, she still had no information she could use to jettison him from the Chatsfield. But she wasn't giving up yet. There were still people she hadn't heard from. And then there was the last email that she'd received from Sara Norrington, the private detective she'd hired to investigate Christos. Sara had said that she was on to something but had refused to share any information until she had something concrete. A little tendril of guilt wrapped around Lucilla's heart but she ignored it. What was there to feel guilty about? She wasn't going to maim him, for God's sake. She just wanted him to resign and move on to the next company.

She gripped her tablet to her chest and leveled a cool gaze on him. He made her insides flutter, damn him. "Did you need something from me?"

One eyebrow lifted and heat slid over her skin. *Oh, heavens...* Talk about a loaded question.

She expected him to remark on it, but he did not. Rather, he spoke imperiously, as if he'd never had his tongue in her mouth and his hands on her body. "Only to remind you that the shareholders' meeting is next week, and we will be leaving immediately after."

It was as if the kiss had never happened, and for some reason that irritated her. She would at least like to know he'd spent half as much time thinking about it as she had. Not that she ever would know it. He'd left that night as he'd arrived: with his supermodel on his arm. Laughing at her, no doubt, for being so flustered when Jessie caught them.

"I know that."

"Though you have not bothered to reply to my email."

She got the distinct feeling he wanted to irritate her. It was working, too. "What is there to reply to? You sent a detailed itinerary. I assumed I was to salute sharply and click my heels."

"Yet a reply in the affirmative is expected. If I assumed that all my memos were received and agreed to without confirmation, I wouldn't be much of an executive, now would I?"

"Then I shall have Jessie respond immediately."

"See that you do."

"You could have just called," she said as he turned away. How dare he show up and put her on the spot, then walk away as if nothing disturbed him?

He pivoted back to her. "You didn't answer your phone. I wasn't prepared to assume you would answer a follow-up."

"I've been busy."

His eyes gleamed. "As have I. Which makes this meeting damned inconvenient, I assure you."

Now he was just making her mad. "So why didn't you pick up the phone and call my office? You know the number. Or, better yet, have your assistant call my assistant. You didn't have to disrupt your excruciatingly *busy* day to come find me."

He glanced over her shoulder, presumably at the kitchen staff who were busily going about their duties peeling vegetables, preparing dishes, washing pots and generally prepping the kitchen for the evening service. No doubt they were paying attention keenly as Lucilla was well aware that both their voices had risen as the conversation went on.

"It seems as if we are attracting attention, Ms. Chatsfield. Would you care to continue this discussion in my office?"

She swallowed. If she refused him, she would look weak to whoever was watching. If she accepted, she would then be alone with Christos. She didn't want to be alone with him. Not because she didn't trust herself, but because it was damned humiliating. She'd spent the past two weeks thinking of his body pressed against hers, his arms wrapped around her. Clearly, he'd been troubled by no such thoughts.

Still, there was only one choice. This was her hotel, damn him. Her birthright.

"Of course," she replied, sweeping past him so that he had to follow her from the kitchen. She hurried down the hallways, aware of him behind her, aware of eyes on them as they swept through the offices. She had no idea if Jessie had repeated what she'd seen that night of the gala, but Lucilla was always conscious of the possibility. Jessie was a good assistant, but all it took was one stray comment and the whole thing could explode like a wildfire. That was simply the nature of office gossip.

Lucilla marched past Christos's assistant, Sophie, just back from her excursion to Chatsfield House, and into his office, turning when she heard the door click shut behind her. Her pulse tripped and stumbled as she tried to maintain her cool.

"I prefer if you do not challenge me in front of the staff," he ground out before she could speak. "It sets a bad precedent."

"Then don't come into my territory to chastise me

in front of *my* staff," she grated back. "Because I will not tolerate it."

His eyes narrowed. "You will not tolerate it? Have you forgotten who is in charge here, Ms. Chatsfield?"

Ms. Chatsfield. He'd called her that twice now when he never had before. For some reason, it annoyed her. Not that she missed being called his Lucilla but, well, dammit…

Lucilla closed her eyes for a second. She didn't know what she missed or why she was irritated. She only knew it was different and she didn't like it. But then she didn't like being called Lucilla *mou,* either.

Argh! What was the matter with her?

"You are not in charge of *me,* Christos. I will respect the fact my father hired you, and I will respect the fact that you even believe you are doing a good job—but I won't be talked down to in front of the staff and I won't keep silent when you irritate me. You are not a god, and this is not your personal domain."

His eyes glittered with heat. And then he laughed. "You amuse me, Lucilla. So much. If you were anyone else, I'd have fired you the first day."

Pleasure suffused her at his use of her name. And then anger, because she wasn't going to be flattered by his admission that she amused him, dammit. The last sentence was the part she needed to focus on. His arrogance was insupportable. "You could have tried. You would not have succeeded."

"Oh, I don't know. I could order the locks rekeyed. How would you get in your office then?"

"I'm sure I would have found a way."

His gaze raked over her. She was wearing a button-down dress today, with long sleeves and a high neck, but he made her feel as if she were in a negligee and little else. "Yes, perhaps you would have."

"Is there anything else you wish to discuss?" she snapped. "I have work to do."

He thrust his hands in his pockets and ranged toward her. Her pulse ticked up a level. He was wearing a gray suit with a white shirt that was unbuttoned a couple of buttons. He rarely wore a tie. Which was annoying because she often found herself focusing on that narrow slice of skin revealed in the opening of his shirt.

"I wonder if you've thought of it at all."

Her throat went dry. "Thought of what?"

"You. Me. A bed. Or a desk. I don't much care."

She felt as if she should utter a shocked gasp, yet all that seemed to be happening was a flood of moisture into her core. Her nipples tightened and she feared he would notice. Her dress was silk—not the most forgiving of fabrics when it came to lumps and bumps beneath the surface.

She brought her tablet up instinctively and hugged it. "I've not thought a thing about it."

It was a lie, of course. She'd thought of little else, especially at night when she climbed into her bed alone.

"I don't believe you, Lucilla *mou*."

And there it was, an annoying flush of pleasure that accompanied his use of her name. Dammit.

"Believe what you like, Christos. Now did you need anything important, or can I get back to work?"

"Ah, but this *is* very important." He stepped closer still, until his scent wrapped around her senses. She trembled at his nearness but did not retreat.

"This is harassment. I could report you."

He gently tugged on the tablet and placed it to one

side, revealing her erect nipples beneath the silk. His gaze clashed with hers then. "And what would you say? That I excite you? That you want to feel my body moving inside yours?"

"That might very well be true," she said softly. "But it's impossible."

It was his turn to swallow. His voice was hoarse when he spoke. "It doesn't need to be impossible. It's sex, Lucilla. Amazing, hot, incredible sex."

She believed him. Oh, God, she believed him—and she wanted it so much even though she wasn't supposed to. "I don't like you." She closed her eyes and shook her head. "I shouldn't want this. I shouldn't want *you*."

"But you do."

"It doesn't matter," she forced out. "It's not happening."

"Why not? We are adults, are we not?"

"You know why."

"I'm afraid I don't."

She flung her arms wide. "Because it would feel like giving up!"

"Giving up what, Lucilla? Loneliness? An empty bed?"

"Who says my bed is empty? I have plenty of sex, I'll have you know. All the time. Just like you and that… that skinny twig of a woman."

He looked puzzled. And then understanding hit him. "Ah, you mean Victoria. Jealous, sweet Lucilla?"

She huffed. "Of course not. What's there to be jealous of? Just because one *can* wear a rubber dress doesn't mean one *should*."

He laughed. "I like that you are jealous. It means you care."

She wanted to thwack him upside the head. And she wanted to wrap her arms around him and kiss him again. "I *don't* care! I despise you! You're a vile, rotten, evil man with a sexy smile and a hot body and it matters not one whit that I want to have sex with you repeatedly—"

She broke off when she realized what she was saying. The look in his eyes was intense.

"Repeatedly. I like the sound of that."

"I misspoke."

He reached for her then, tugged her into his arms, and she wrapped her fists in his lapels—whether to tug him closer or push him away, she wasn't sure.

"Lucilla," he murmured, his lips against her ear. "You drive me crazy."

"Oh," she said as his mouth moved along her throat. "Oh, don't do that."

"Why not?" His voice was a sexy rumble against her skin.

Because it felt too good. Because liquid heat was flooding into her sex and she was afraid of what she might do if this bone-deep need didn't ease soon.

"Christos…" she sighed as his lips moved over her collarbone. "We can't…"

"We can."

He picked her up and sat her on his desk—and her heart began to gallop. She felt dizzy and drunk and she knew she was on the edge of a decision that would change everything.

He stepped between her legs, cupping her face in both his hands. She wanted his kiss more than she wanted her next breath. But she couldn't allow it, couldn't surrender to him like this.

Christos tilted her head back and her eyes closed

as she anticipated his lips touching hers. She called up a picture of Jessie walking in on them and ice water dripped into her veins, giving her strength.

She pushed him away, scrambling off the desk to face him. Disappointment ate at her like acid. But she'd done the right thing, dammit. "I won't be an object of office gossip. I won't have them know—"

He seemed to stiffen, as if she'd insulted him. "Of course not. That would not be seemly. The Chatsfield princess and the Greek."

He made it sound dirty, as if she thought she was too good for him. "That's not what I mean and you know it."

"Do I?"

"You don't stay, Christos. You come in, fix whatever needs to be fixed and move on to the next high-powered job. But this is my birthright and I will remain. I won't have anyone thinking I slept my way into the CEO job when it's finally mine."

His eyes flashed with irritation. "Confident it'll be yours, aren't you?"

She thrust her chin out. "Yes." She would be even more so when Sara came up with the goods on him.

"This is what I like about you, Lucilla. You don't back down from a challenge."

"No, I don't." She picked up her tablet and clutched it like a shield again.

"And yet you do run away from them sometimes. When they are too personal."

She trembled. She hated that he knew that about her, that he could see it. Was she that predictable? That obvious? She'd given up so many things for so long—she'd even given up a personal life while she'd worked her ass off to make this company prosper, but she was currently little more than a glorified employee. Still fighting. Still working to prove herself.

And she couldn't stop that fight. Not yet, and not over something so simple as hormones. She wanted him, but she couldn't have him. It was too dangerous. When he touched her, she forgot that. When he did not, she could think straight again.

"I'm not running. Not all battles are worth the fight."

His eyes narrowed and she knew she'd scored a direct hit. It bothered her that he thought she was a snob, but if that's what it took to make him keep his distance…

"Of course not." Christos took a step backward, and then another. "But ask yourself, Lucilla *mou,* when you touch yourself tonight, how much better it would have been if I were the one caressing you instead."

Her heart slammed against her ribs. Need—such wild, wild need—speared into her. There was nothing she could say, no way she could deny that powerful image he'd placed in her head.

"Please leave." Her vocal chords were tight.

"But this is my office," he said softly, mockingly.

A lightning bolt of shame and fresh hate sizzled into her. She'd been right to push him away. *So right.* She marched to the door, then stopped and threw him a look over her shoulder. "Not forever, it isn't. That much I promise you."

CHAPTER FOUR

CHRISTOS WORKED LATE and then went home. But he was too restless to settle in, so he walked down the street to a Greek takeout and picked up dinner for two. His plan was to go home and call one of the women in his contact list. A leisurely dinner, some wine, a little love-making—just what he needed to get his mind off Lucilla Chatsfield.

Infuriating, sexy Lucilla. He'd been attracted to her almost from the beginning—but his desire for her had grown over the past few weeks. It had happened slowly at first, and then, when he'd seen her in that red dress at the auction, he'd realized just how intensely he wanted her.

She didn't simper and bat her eyelashes at him. She didn't care how big his bank account was. She would cheerfully wish him to the devil if she could—and yet she wanted him. She'd admitted as much today.

When he thought of her nipples beaded tight against the silk of her dress, he grew hard. He would have taken her on her desk if she'd given him the chance. Just like two weeks ago, before her assistant had walked in on them.

Damn her for being so infuriatingly stubborn. He'd

been surprised when she'd pushed him away—and then he'd been uncharacteristically hurt, though he told himself it was ridiculous to be so. She did not know his background, did not know she was pushing his buttons pretty hard. All she knew was how scared she was of what might happen if she gave in.

He meant to go home, but he found himself walking in the opposite direction. The wind picked up and the clouds grew darker. Soon, it would rain, and he'd be soaked to the skin. He almost welcomed it, if it would help to cool this heat in his blood.

But it didn't rain, though the air was thick with the promise of it. Eventually he found himself on the street in front of her building; he couldn't quite believe it had been his destination all along. But it had.

He walked up to the door and hit the bell for her apartment.

Her voice came on the intercom a few moments later. "Yes?"

"Have you eaten?"

He heard the intake of her breath. "Christos? It's nine o'clock! What are you doing here?"

"Asking if you've eaten, or if you worked late and skipped dinner."

She paused. "I ate an apple."

"Not good enough, Lucilla. You need real food. Tonight, I am your delivery boy."

"You brought dinner?" He could hear the surprise in her voice.

"Yes."

"Confident, aren't you?" she asked, echoing his own words from earlier back to him.

"Not at all," he told her truthfully. "But I am here and

I've brought an offering. Let me in, fair Lucilla, or banish me. Your choice."

"I'm angry with you."

"I know this. I brought a peace offering."

She didn't answer. But the door buzzed as she freed the lock and Christos went inside.

Lucilla's heart turned over. She glanced in the mirror by her apartment door and frowned. She'd come home and changed into yoga pants and a soft T-shirt so she could curl up on the sofa and read the reports from her staff.

She had not expected company. She had certainly not expected Christos. She heard his footsteps on the stairs and yanked the door open. He was still wearing his suit from earlier, and his hair was gorgeously tousled from the breeze outside. He came up the last step and stopped. Then he held up a bag.

"Souvlaki, pita, rice, dolmades and baklava."

Lucilla blinked. "Don't tell me you cook."

"I do, actually. But I didn't cook this. Still, I promise it's good."

She pulled the door wider and he came inside, smelling like the night air and something spicy, too. She closed it behind him and then headed for the kitchen because she did not know what to say. When she got there, she began to pull out plates and silverware. Christos took the food from the bag and set the containers in a row on her island.

It was almost companionable, which seemed strange considering they were enemies.

Enemies who were powerfully attracted to each other, apparently. So attracted that she'd gone against every bit of good sense she possessed and let him in.

She spied the bottle of wine she'd planned to open earlier. She'd been texting Antonio and forgot all about it. A sliver of guilt threatened to prick her as she remembered what they'd been texting about.

Christos. Specifically, getting rid of Christos.

"Wine?" she asked, picking up the bottle. Because she certainly needed it now.

Christos flashed her a smile that made her insides quiver. "Sounds good."

She fished in the cabinet for the opener. But her hands were trembling too much to do a proper job and she swore softly as she failed to get the corkscrew seated for the second time.

"Here, let me." Christos was beside her, his big body almost startling as he invaded her space. He took the corkscrew from her hands, took the bottle, too, and then deftly inserted the device. She watched as he expertly worked the cork free.

"You must have been a waiter once."

He lifted an eyebrow. "Indeed. Though not for long."

"Didn't like it, huh?"

His expression was coolly amused. "No, I bought the restaurant."

She should have known. "You went from being a waiter to being the owner. How long did that take?"

"Six months."

Lucilla wanted to whistle. "You do have a hell of a reputation, Christos."

That much was certainly true. Everything she'd learned about him since she'd started researching him only made him seem more formidable—and yes, even somewhat supernatural—than before. Christos achieved things that others could not. He did not fail, and he did not leave a business in worse shape than when he arrived. He always improved upon what he'd been given.

She knew that—and yet she knew she could do the same thing, at least where the Chatsfield empire was concerned. She knew the business backward and forward because she'd worked pretty much every position in the hotels there was, from chambermaid to front desk and beyond. She'd been preparing for it her entire adult life, but her father didn't have faith in her ability.

It still stung, even after all these weeks, and she bit down on the bitter flood of acid in her throat. Thinking about her father would only make her angry and upset, and she'd prefer to keep her wits about her. She had a very dark, very handsome, very dangerous man in her kitchen.

And she still had no idea why he was here. Or why she'd let him in.

Christos stood so near, his scent wrapping around her, invading her senses. He handed her a glass of wine, clinking his with hers. "It's because I deliver on my promises," he said, sipping the wine. "*All* of them."

And there it was again, that liquid slide of heat infusing her limbs. Weakening her with longing. She never knew when it was going to hit, but it seemed to do so way too often of late.

It made her grumpy. "How do you manage to make everything you say sound as if it has a double meaning?"

He laughed. "Perhaps because it does."

"Why are you here, Christos?"

His eyes glittered hot. "For the same reason you let me in, Lucilla *mou*."

Heat spread over her skin like an incoming tide. "I let you in because you had food."

"Of course." He set his wine down and shed his suit jacket. Her heart nearly stopped in her chest as she wondered what he might do next—but he only rolled up his sleeves, revealing powerful forearms, and then picked up a plate and dished out some food. "Here, try these dolmades. You will think you are in heaven."

Lucilla blinked. How could he think of food right now when all she could think of was heat and skin and sex? He'd put that thought in her head, damn him. She had *not* let him in for any other reason than because he'd brought dinner.

Riiightt...

Lucilla shook off her incriminating thoughts and joined him at the island. She slipped onto a barstool and speared a grape leaf stuffed with mint, rice and lamb. It was delicious, slightly warm, and she quickly took another bite.

"It's fabulous," she said, surprised at how hungry she was. She often ate something small in the evenings, but even she had to admit that an apple wasn't quite enough. She'd been busy and she'd put off getting up and rummaging in the refrigerator for something more when the doorbell rang.

"Yes, it is. Did you try the souvlaki yet?"

She stabbed a bit of the spiced lamb. "Oh, wow, it melts in your mouth."

His eyes narrowed as he watched her chew and she suddenly felt hot again. Outside, a bolt of lightning flashed across the sky.

"Indeed it does."

They ate in silence for a few moments while outside the sky rumbled and cracked. Lucilla studied the food on her plate rather than looking at Christos.

Dammit, this was silly. She was a grown woman, not a teenager with a crush. She could look at him. Just lift her head and—

He was watching her, his blue eyes warm and deep as an ocean for a change. The heat flashing through her grew hotter.

"Don't stare at me," she said.

He took a leisurely drink of his wine. "Why not? You are beautiful. I like looking at you."

"I'm not one of your conquests, Christos. Save the compliments."

He shrugged and set his wine down again. "Tell me why you are so different from your siblings."

Her heart thumped. "I'm not sure what you mean."

"You're very serious, very studious. Your name is never linked with scandal. You've had no embarrassing entanglements, no public meltdowns. And you don't seem to want attention. In fact, you shrink from it. I compliment you and you get angry."

Lucilla didn't know what to say. A ball of emotion rolled in the pit of her stomach. It shouldn't surprise her that he knew things about her, but it somehow did.

Worse, he'd observed things that no amount of research could have told him. Like her inability to accept compliments. To her, they always seemed like false promises. Things people said in order to deflect you from the fact they weren't going to be there for you when you needed them. She didn't need compliments when she had accomplishments.

Lucilla dragged in a breath. There were some things she didn't like to talk about, some hurts that went too deep. Inside, she would always be the little girl who wasn't lovable enough. Her mother had left them all, and her father had happily let her and Antonio take on the task of raising their siblings while he'd caroused in London. He'd never thanked them for it, either.

Her coping mechanism had always been to be the good girl. Because how could her parents fail to love the good girl? If she were good enough, she'd thought, maybe her mother would come back.

She took a swallow of her wine. Oh, she knew what a naive thought that was now. But as a girl, it had been very defining. Her entire life had revolved around that thought for so long that it was ingrained in her.

"Not every Chatsfield needs attention," she said softly. "Perhaps I'm one who does not. And I can accept compliments. I just prefer them to have meaning rather than be a means to an end."

"And who says my compliment has no meaning? You? I assure you that you are very beautiful indeed. I want you, Lucilla. I think you know this."

"How do I know you aren't just saying it?" Because he was a spider on a web, a puppet master dangling the strings—he'd managed everyone thus far. What if he was managing her, too? Managing her with the things she needed most—companionship and belonging.

"I thought I proved that already."

She snorted. "An erection? All you need do is close your eyes and think of rubber-dress girl and you're there. I'm not so stupid I don't get that trick."

He looked incredulous. And then he reached for her hand, threaded his fingers in hers and raised it to press his lips to the skin on the inside of her wrist. A shiver ricocheted through her. "Believe me when I tell you that the only reason I might think of her when I'm with you is to *calm* a raging erection. Not the other way around."

"You are such a liar," she breathed.

His eyes were intense. "I dare you to test me, Lucilla. Take me to your bedroom and test me."

Her heart skipped wildly. She couldn't answer that challenge. "Tell me you didn't sleep with her. I bet you can't."

He shook his head. "No, I can't."

"I knew it."

"And what has this to do with you and me and right now?"

Another bolt of lightning flashed outside the window and the lights flickered. She extracted her hand. "I won't be a conquest. I see no point in it."

He stabbed another bite of lamb and chewed it. "Really? This from the woman who's been having lots and lots of sex?"

Her color rose. "I don't need you if I'm getting off with other men, do I?"

"I'm better than they are, Lucilla."

"You are *so* arrogant."

"No, just truthful. If I were your lover, you wouldn't be getting excited by another man the way you are with me." He grinned. "These lovers are inadequate."

Her ears were hot. But the wine was working its magic, making her feel languid and relaxed for the first time in days. Outside, the rain came down hard. Inside, she felt warm and cozy and even a tiny bit content. "Maybe I'm just insatiable."

He dropped his fork and groaned. "Don't put that thought in my head. It makes my imagination run wild."

She wanted to ask what kinds of things he was imagining. But that was a very bad idea. Lucilla took another sip of wine. "If you were anyone else…"

"And who is the liar now, Lucilla?" His voice was soft and mocking—but not in a mean way. In a way that made her insides curl and twist.

"I don't know what you mean."

"I think you do." He leaned forward and caressed her cheek. "For all your talk, you are a workaholic. You work late, you go home alone every night and you come in early every day. You aren't having sex with anyone, insatiably or otherwise."

She wanted to deny it. But there was really no point. "It's not polite to call a girl a liar."

"No? I didn't think politeness was one of my strong points, anyway."

"It definitely isn't. Besides, if you knew I wasn't having sex with anyone, why did you take such pains to tell me how much better you are than my imaginary lovers?"

He laughed, and the warmth of the sound slid down her spine. "Did you think I would pass up an opportunity to tell you how good I could make you feel?" He shook his head. "Not a chance."

"You really are full of yourself."

"There's one way to find out, isn't there?"

She crossed her arms and leaned back on the stool. "You never stop trying to bait me into it, do you?"

"I'm a man. It's what we do when we want a woman."

His words made her shiver deep inside. Oh, how she wanted to just let go and see where this could lead. It had been so long since any man had touched her that she was almost willing to throw caution to the wind and let Christos be the one to break the long drought.

"Maybe we should talk about something else for a while," she said, desperate to change the subject before she climbed in his lap or did something equally outrageous.

"What do you wish to discuss?"

"I don't know. Tell me about your life. Tell me why you came to London when you could be lounging on a beach in Greece."

"If I were lounging on a beach in Greece, I would not be very successful, now would I?"

"You could afford to lounge a bit, I'm sure. Aren't you already successful?" He'd built up a pretty amazing fortune, according to her sources. Yet here he was, working for her father. Except that wasn't quite true. Christos was like a rock star of the corporate world. He commanded a very high price and what he did could hardly be called working for anyone.

He worked for himself. When he was satisfied he'd done all he could, he moved on and took the next challenge someone presented him with.

"I am. But if I were to lounge on beaches, as you suggest, I wouldn't have the sort of work ethic conducive to being successful."

She snorted. "Surely you can take a vacation here and there."

His eyes were unfathomable. "I don't need a vacation, Lucilla *mou*. I need to work."

"It sounds very tiring."

He lifted an eyebrow. "And when did you last take a vacation?"

"Last year. I took a long weekend and went to Spain."

"To the Chatsfield Preitalle, yes?"

She was silent for a long moment. "Yes."

He shook his head. "You are every bit as bad as I am.

And I like this about you. Unlike the rest of your siblings, you understand how to work."

She propped an elbow on the island and leaned on it. "I thought I was spoiled."

"You are. But that doesn't mean you haven't learned the value of hard work."

"Sometimes you make no sense, Christos."

He straightened. "It makes perfect sense. You work because the Chatsfield means something to you. But you've never *had* to really work."

She would not tell him about tending to Nicolo when he'd been in agony after his accident. There'd been a time when she was the only person Nicolo would let near him, and that had meant a lot of sleepless nights in addition to full days of care. Sadly, Nicolo didn't let anyone near these days. It worried her, but he was a grown man now and he would do things in his own time.

And then there was Cara, who'd been a baby when their mother had walked out. Lucilla knew what it was like to work to raise a child, even though the child had not technically been hers. Oh, yes, she knew all about work, but she wasn't going to tell Christos these things. They were none of his business.

"I'll have you know I was a chambermaid for a month." She said it coolly, proudly.

He snorted. "Yes, but always with the understanding that you could stop at any time. That you would not go hungry if you did. You've never had to do things to *survive,* Lucilla. That is the difference."

She could only stare at him. At his handsome face and high cheekbones, at the way his eyes flashed. And she understood something about him that she never had before. It made her heart twist in sympathy. "You did, didn't you?"

"Yes."

She reached for his hand impulsively, squeezed his fingers. He was looking at her curiously, as if she was a rare species and he had to be very quiet or scare her away.

"I'm sorry these things happened to you."

She felt him tense beneath her touch. "Nothing terrible happened to me, *glykia mou*. I had to work hard or I wouldn't have had money to eat. That's not a bad thing. It's a very normal thing for anyone not born into privilege."

She swallowed. She'd felt close to him for just a second, like she understood something about him, but he'd just proven to her that she understood nothing. No, she'd never had to worry about her next meal or the roof over her head. But she had lived without much affection, and that seemed to be a poor existence indeed.

Christos would not agree, she was certain. She pulled her hand away and folded it in her lap, suddenly self-conscious.

He tipped her chin up with a finger and she found herself looking into deep, dark blue eyes. "Careful, Lucilla," he said softly. "I might think you care."

She sucked in a breath, steadied herself. "Well, I don't. I was just being polite."

He laughed. "You seem to do that a lot."

"Be polite? It's the way I was raised."

"And I was raised to say what I think and take what I want."

Her heart thumped against her chest wall. "We can't always have what we want, Christos."

He stroked a finger down her cheek, over the column of her neck. Her skin prickled. "Why can't we?"

She licked her lips as need and fear twined together in her belly. "Because sometimes it's a very bad idea."

His gaze dipped to where her pulse beat in her throat, back up again. His eyes glittered with heat and promise. The lights flickered and she wondered insanely if he were somehow in control of them.

"Sometimes. But sometimes it's a very good idea. What if this is one of those times?"

CHAPTER FIVE

CHRISTOS WATCHED HER throat move as she swallowed. Her pulse tripped along like a trapped butterfly's wings. He wanted, very much, to press his mouth there and feel the beat of her heart. He felt the compulsion as fiercely as the storm raging outside, but he would not do so without her invitation.

"I don't know how you can say that," she said. But she picked up the wine with trembling fingers and he hid a smile of satisfaction. She was not unaffected by this pull between them. That, at least, was gratifying.

"Passion, *glykia mou*. It is all about passion. Our passion might spring from intense…disagreement, but it is still passion."

She arched an eyebrow then. "I can't imagine how you see an affair between us going. Won't your style be cramped when I don't conveniently disappear from your life the next morning? You'll have to face me over a conference table on a regular basis. It will be awkward."

"You're making excuses, Lucilla. We don't know what it will be like until we've traveled that path, do we?"

"I'm still not convinced." She pulled in a breath and stood, gathering plates and silverware. "I can't even believe you have me thinking about this. Earlier today, if

I could have vaporized you with a look, I would have happily done so."

That made him laugh. Because it wasn't the usual reaction he got from women. "Then I should be thankful you cannot."

He stood and began to help her by closing up the containers again. They worked in silence, moving the dishes to the sink and the food to the refrigerator. When she walked away from the sink, he went over and started the water running.

"What are you doing?"

He slanted her a look. "Washing dishes."

Her jaw dropped. "You can't be serious."

"Why not?" He nodded toward the sink. "They're dirty, aren't they?"

"I was planning to get them in the morning. Besides, it's storming. What if we lose power?"

"Then the dishes will be half done. But at least we can try."

Probably she had a maid come in and tidy up for her, but he didn't know that for certain. He'd learned the pleasures of having domestic help a long time ago, but he was still capable of cleaning up a mess here and there.

She came around and grabbed a towel while he began to wash. There wasn't much—a couple of plates, knives, forks and the spoons they'd dipped the food out with—and it didn't take long. She closed the last cabinet and set the towel down.

"I can't believe you washed my dishes. I should have taken a video so I could post it online."

He leaned against the sink and crossed his arms. "And do what? Prove that I wash dishes sometimes? Scandalous information indeed."

Her face lit with mischief. "Ah, but if I pointed out they were *my* dishes and you were secretly my love slave, this could be detrimental to your reputation. Women everywhere would wail and rend their garments. Men would no longer respect you in the boardroom."

She made him laugh. "What you fail to grasp, sweet Lucilla, is that I don't really care what anyone thinks of me. So long as the job gets done—and it will—they can believe I wear ladies' underwear in the privacy of my own home and paint my nails on weekends."

Her jaw was slack. "Do you?"

He was almost offended. After he'd just told her he didn't care, he *did* care when it was Lucilla wondering these things. He straightened to his full height and, gripping her forearms, tugged her against him. She was soft and warm, her body lushly curved. She did not pull away—nor did she push him. Her hands came up to rest on his shirt, but lightly.

He knew the tide could turn, knew she could push him away a moment later, but he was going to take full advantage of her cooperation right this second.

"The only ladies' underwear I'm interested in is yours," he growled. "And I don't want to wear it so much as rip it off your body."

Her breath hitched in. "I still think it's a bad idea."

"It's only your brain that thinks that, Lucilla. Your body has a very different idea."

She dropped her gaze and studied her hands where they rested on his chest. Then she drew in a breath. He could feel her surrender before she said the words. "I know."

She was supposed to be the good girl. She was supposed to do everything right, be strong and come out on top at the end of the day. But here she was with Christos Giatrakos, the man she was working hard to topple, and all she could think about was how good it felt to be pressed up against him, her body melting into the hard angles of his.

He was spectacular, damn him. Her brain might resist, but her body knew it and wanted more.

She put her forehead against his chest and concentrated on breathing. He skimmed his fingers up and down her spine, his touch comforting and titillating at the same time. She could feel the tension building inside her as he continued to stroke her. But he made no move to take the moment deeper and her stomach began to twist with need and frustration.

She *wanted* him to do something. Wanted him to be the one to make the first move so she could tell herself later that she'd been a victim of her hormones. That she'd operated on instinct rather than making a conscious decision.

But all he continued to do was hold her while her nerves tightened.

"I don't understand this," she said. "I'd just as soon see you drive off into the sunset as spend another moment watching you sit at my desk and issue orders like a potentate."

His voice was a rumble in her ear. "It drives you crazy, yes? Me in charge..."

She tilted her head back to look up at him. "You know it does."

"And what will you do when I take charge in bed, Lucilla?"

A shudder rippled over her. "Perhaps I won't allow it."

His eyes glittered. "Ah, another battleground, then.

I have a feeling it will be a most pleasurable and explosive battle."

She curled her fingers in his shirt. "Why is everything a battle with you?"

"Who says it is?"

"You have a fierce need to conquer, Christos. I've watched you do it a hundred times in a hundred different meetings. You make everything into a battle."

His brows drew down. He looked reflective. "Perhaps this is true. And yet I do not wish to battle you tonight. Yes, I wish to conquer. But in a good way. In a most exciting way."

"Why can't we conquer each other?"

"Perhaps we can." He bent toward her then, dipped his mouth to her collarbone. Lucilla closed her eyes and sucked in a sharp gasp as his lips and tongue moved over her skin. Oh, she was insane to allow it. Insane to even contemplate going to bed with Christos.

"I wish I understood what this is," she said on a sigh.

He lifted his head to look at her. "It's sex, Lucilla."

"I realize that. What I mean is *why*. Why you?"

"You keep asking this, and there is no answer. It simply is."

She frowned. "That implies we aren't in charge of our choices."

He looked puzzled. "This *is* a choice. I'm here. You're here."

She pushed him back when he would have bent to kiss her again. "And if I wanted you to leave?"

He didn't hesitate. "Then I'll go."

Somehow, she didn't want that, either. She let out a frustrated growl. It was damned inconvenient to want the man you desperately wanted to destroy. "Wouldn't you be happier if I offered my resignation and went on a pilgrimage to Tibet or something?"

"It might make my task at the Chatsfield easier, but the truth is I wouldn't wish you anywhere else."

"You say the damnedest things sometimes, Christos."

He pulled her tighter to him, until she could feel all the contours of his body against hers. Hard contours, solid contours. *Oh, my...*

She'd admired his body for weeks, slid surreptitious looks in his direction when he wasn't watching—her and every other red-blooded female on the staff—and envied the women on his arm, though she knew she should not. It annoyed her a great deal to envy them, but she'd told herself it was simply because he *did* look like a Greek god and it was okay to appreciate that from afar.

His hands slid down her back, over her hips. She thought he would kiss her but he did not. He looked at her very seriously while her heartbeat raced and moist heat slid between her breasts. "This is when you need to tell me to leave," he said.

"I know." She dragged in a breath. She didn't want him to let her go. But what choice did she have? She was so accustomed to denying herself that it came more naturally than the alternative. She dropped her hands from his chest and took a step back. "I—I think you should go."

"Do you really? Or do you just think you should say so?"

She curled her hands into fists. Outside, rain slashed against the windows. "You must understand. I can't sleep with you, Christos. Even though I want to."

He speared her with a look. "Very well." Then he

went and grabbed his jacket from the back of the chair, slinging it over his arm.

Disappointment swirled inside her. She felt almost desperate with it. "Do you want the leftovers?"

"You keep them."

He took his phone out as he walked toward the door. And that was the moment when she felt as if she would never be close to anyone again, as if everything she'd ever sacrificed had been for naught. She was lonely, isolated in her ivory tower of duty and devotion to her family and her career. When was it okay to take something for herself?

When that something isn't the one person standing between you and success.

Dammit. Lucilla pulled in a deep breath as he reached the door. He stopped and shrugged into his jacket. And then he was looking at her again, those deep blue eyes searching hers. He reached out and slipped his hand along her jaw. "It was fun for once, Lucilla *mou*. No arguments, no anger. Perhaps we can get along, after all, yes?"

Impulsively, she put her hand over his where it rested on her jaw. "I doubt it. You'll make me angry tomorrow before I've had my first cup of coffee. But it *was* pleasant."

He smiled and her heart turned over. God, why did he have to be so unbelievably beautiful for a man? "I'm glad to hear you admit it."

The lights flickered again, longer this time, and she looked up at the fixture. Christos was looking, too. "It's quite a storm," she whispered.

"Yes."

"You don't even have an umbrella."

"Do you care if I get wet?"

She shrugged. "Not really. And if you could manage to get struck by lightning, that would really help me out."

His eyes widened. And then he laughed. "Bloodthirsty little thing, aren't you?"

She gripped his forearm. "I'm kidding, Christos. I'd like you to go away, but alive and well and unharmed."

"Well, thank you for that. I think."

"It's definitely a compliment. A month ago, I wouldn't have cared how you went away so long as you did."

"Then I'll count my blessings." He bent and kissed her on the cheek and her heart kicked hard. It was a sweet gesture, nothing sexual, but she found she missed the sexual.

He opened the door and the lights popped out. All the sounds in her apartment—the hum of the refrigerator, the electronic buzz of several appliances—went completely silent.

"You can't leave," she said after a long moment.

He made a movement and a light flared. His phone. "I have a light. And I'll call a cab."

"You didn't drive?"

"No."

"The traffic lights might be out, too. It'll be chaos until they get the power restored." The Chatsfield wasn't far from here, but it had a generator and protocols in place to make sure the guests were not inconvenienced. Her building, however, did not have backup power.

"Are you asking me to stay, Lucilla?"

"Until the power is restored, yes."

"Are you afraid of the dark?"

She snorted. "Hardly." She wasn't afraid of it, precisely, because she'd always made a game of it when they'd lost power at Chatsfield House. But then she'd been surrounded by children and servants. Here?

It wasn't her first power outage, or likely her last, but no, she didn't like being alone when everything was so bloody still.

Christos shut the door again. His phone still gave off a warm glow and she could feel his heat. It was comforting, in a way.

"Well, I'm afraid of the dark," he said matter-of-factly.

"You are not."

He put an arm around her and guided her back toward the kitchen. "No, not really. I just thought it would make you feel happier if you thought I was."

She rolled her eyes. "You don't care if I'm happy or not."

"Maybe I do."

"Please."

"Or maybe I just like it when you smile."

"I smile. A lot."

"Not at me."

"You don't do anything to deserve it, Christos. Now hold the phone up while I check the drawers for candles."

She found candles and a lighter. She lit those and set them on the island, and they returned to the stools they'd occupied not so long ago.

"I like it when you smile," he said, and her heart turned over.

"You *are* smooth. No wonder you've bedded half of London so far."

He snorted. "Half of London? I wasn't aware you'd noticed."

Heat prickled at the back of her neck. "It's impossible not to. If you aren't showing up at Chatsfield functions with a new woman on your arm, you're in the gossip pages with them."

"I have no control over what those rags print."

"None of us do," she said softly.

"You are trying to make a point, I assume?"

"Just that I know the Chatsfields haven't given a good showing lately, but the papers often exaggerate just to make sales."

"I am aware of that."

She felt a pinch in her chest. "Cara is troubled, Christos. But she's not bad. She's not a disgrace."

"I never said she was. I merely sent her where her shenanigans would do the least harm."

"Vegas. Yes." She pictured Cara in Sin City and wondered what the child she'd raised would be getting up to there. It worried her, but Cara was an adult now and not best pleased whenever Lucilla interfered in her life.

"You are worried about her."

It surprised her that he noticed. "Yes. She's so young. And impulsive."

"The young usually are."

He said it in such a way that she found herself studying him, wondering what experiences lurked behind those eyes. "I wasn't."

He snorted. "No, I can certainly believe that."

She had to control her voice not to show her annoyance. "What makes you say that?"

"Lucilla *mou,* if you were in the least bit impulsive, we would have had gotten naked together weeks ago."

Heat slid through her belly. "You're teasing me."

"I am. Somewhat." He picked up the wine he hadn't finished earlier and took a sip. "But it's true. You are not impulsive. You think everything through, often too much."

"I'm not sure I like being analyzed by you."

He shrugged. "You cannot stop me from analyzing you. Only from saying what I find." He leaned toward her, as if daring her to put a hand over his mouth. She did not. "And what I find is that you overthink too many things. Make decisions, Lucilla. Implement them. Learn from your mistakes and don't make the same ones again."

She grew stiff. "You're implying that I'm less of a manager than you and I don't appreciate it one bit."

"This is not what I said. But if it's what you take from my words…" He shrugged.

Her insides clenched tight. "I'm thinking I should have let you stand outside and get soaked. Oh, and the lightning thing? I've changed my mind again."

Christos laughed. "If I were anyone else, you wouldn't feel so insulted. You're good at what you do. I didn't say you weren't. What I said was that you don't go with your gut as often as you should. Sometimes, that's all we have to go on."

She glared at him. "You really annoy me, Christos."

He slid his fingers up the inside of her arm, heat dancing in their wake. "But I excite you, too."

Damn him, it was true. He did excite her. Her skin tingled. Her stomach rose and fell like a boat on a wavy sea. She sniffed. "That's beside the point. You can't insult me and expect I'll fall into your arms."

"Then tell me what it takes and I'll do that."

"You're the expert. Figure it out yourself."

His eyes sparkled with heat and humor. "Since you didn't tell me to go to hell, I'm feeling encouraged."

She poured more wine into her glass and took a drink. The lights had been out for at least fifteen minutes now. Everything in the apartment was still, but outside it still thundered, the rain sheeting down. She could hear the occasional horns of frustrated drivers blaring in the night.

"Lucilla." His voice was soft and she turned to look at him, her heart turning over at the intensity of his gaze. "Don't take everything as an insult. I'm blunt because you're strong enough to hear it. If you weren't, I wouldn't waste my breath on you."

She felt like she should be insulted, and yet part of her was inordinately pleased. "I went to Oxford, Christos. I'm not an idiot."

"You aren't. But I have more experience. You can learn from me. That's all you need to do. Learn. You'll get what you want in the end."

"Have you ever stopped to consider that maybe you could learn something from me?" And just why was she saying this? She wanted him gone, not partnering up with her to run the hotels.

"Of course. But first you have to be willing to work with me."

"I do work with you."

His smile made her heart skip. "No, you fight me. About everything."

"Not everything."

"Yes, everything. If I want blue decorations for an event, you go with red. If I ask for one menu, you change it to another. If I say I want to host this group, you choose that group."

She did do that. She'd never really considered that she

might do it on purpose. "It's not out of spite. I do what is best for the hotel at the time."

He arched an eyebrow. "Do you? Or do you just like to thwart me?"

"I don't get the impression many people thwart you, Christos."

"You do. Continually."

Her heart thumped in her chest. "Well, blind obedience can be so boring."

"You definitely aren't boring, *glykia mou*. Far from it."

"Flattery, Christos," she chided. "It will get you nowhere."

He got to his feet and she tilted her head back to look up at him.

"Yes, I am aware. And I think it's time I go." He put the wineglass down and picked up his phone from where he'd set it on the island. *"Kalispera, glykia mou."*

She shot to her feet, feeling suddenly bereft at the idea of him leaving her sitting here alone. "It's still raining, Christos. And the power is out. You can't leave in this. You won't get home for hours."

"And yet I feel I have overstayed my welcome."

She clenched her hands into fists at her sides. He'd been perfectly pleasant for the most part. She'd been the one who'd had trouble letting go of her animosity— and her fear.

"I'm sorry I've been prickly. You just aggravate me so much. But please stay. I have a guest room, and you are welcome to it for as long as you like."

He took so long to reply that she thought he would refuse. His eyes glittered in the candlelight and she had a sudden urge to slide into his arms and wrap herself around him.

"Very well," he finally said. "I accept your kind offer."

CHAPTER SIX

LUCILLA LAY IN her bed and tried to sleep. It wasn't working. The house was so still. But that wasn't the problem. No, the problem was that Christos was in the next room. They'd talked a little more, about mundane things, and then he'd said he would like to turn in. So she'd shown him to the guest room, given him some candles and retreated to her own room.

That was two hours ago now and she just couldn't fall asleep. She kept thinking about Christos lying so near. He would have stripped down to his underwear. Perhaps he lay on top of the sheets, his body exposed to the night. A dagger of heat stabbed into her when she thought of him almost naked.

Really, it had been too long. Perhaps she needed a trip to the adult toy store. She could buy something with different speeds, keep it wrapped up in the bedside table until needed. She could name it. Not a Greek name. Definitely not a Greek name. Jack. She would call it Jack, and Jack would ease this ache she felt whenever her body insisted on remembering the way Christos kissed her.

Lucilla groaned and put her pillow over her face. This was ridiculous. Her cheeks were hot just thinking about setting foot inside an adult store. Not that there was anything wrong with it, but she could hardly walk inside one and browse. Maybe online. Yes, online. She could do that....

A noise penetrated her lust-crazed thoughts, instantly sobering her. Had someone said something? She sat up in bed and strained to hear. And then she heard it again, a masculine cry coming from the bedroom next to hers. Alarm prickled her skin. Goose bumps rose along her arms. She got up and whipped on a robe, then grabbed her phone and turned on its light app before going out into the hallway.

Christos cried out again and she hurried over to the door and knocked. The sound stopped abruptly.

"Christos? Is everything all right? Christos!"

The door whipped open a few seconds later. He stood there exactly as she'd known he would be dressed— wearing a pair of dark briefs and nothing else. Lucilla swallowed. His chest was bare and glistening, as if he'd been working out. His hair was mussed—and his eyes were wild.

He swallowed, as if trying to get control of himself. "I'm fine."

She hugged herself, suddenly unsure. "I'm sorry to intrude. I just heard... I thought..." She couldn't finish the sentence. What had she thought? That he was having a bad dream? Clearly.

He raked a hand through his hair. "It happens sometimes. It's nothing."

"Do you want to talk?"

His eyebrows lifted. "Talk? No, I don't want to talk. If you have another offer, I'll entertain that. But talking? Hell, no."

"I—I'm sorry I disturbed you." She backed up a step, intent on turning and going back to her room.

Christos said something in Greek. And then he reached for her, tugged her into his arms. She went willingly, which was a bit of a shock—and not a shock, in a way.

"I'm sorry," he said hoarsely. "Just let me hold you, yes? That's what I need right now."

She put her arms around him. They stood there for a few minutes, her head against his chest, his chin resting on her hair. His heart thundered and she found herself smoothing her hands over his back, trying to soothe him. She'd raised children and she knew that they often just needed to be held after a nightmare.

She had no idea what could make a man like Christos yell in his sleep, but it must be frightening to him. Dammit, she didn't want to like him. Not even a little bit. But knowing he was human, that he had fears and frailties, too, could not fail to put a chink in her heart.

"You should go back to bed," he finally said.

"I wasn't sleeping, anyway."

He pushed her away just a little and she tilted her head back to look up at him. What she saw in his gaze made her heart flip. His eyes glittered with heat and need. "Go, *glykia mou,* before I kiss you. Because if I kiss you, I won't stop there."

She knew she should step back, walk away. But she couldn't seem to make her feet move. Not when her body was melting against his, not when there was a white-hot fire burning low in her belly, not when he looked as lost and alone as she so often felt.

"Kiss me, then," she said, her voice as raspy and hoarse as his had been only a moment ago.

He uttered something in Greek before he brought his mouth down on hers—and the fire that had been simmering between them exploded in a flash of heat.

It was late and dark, the kind of hour where secrets rose to the surface and desires could no longer be contained. Lucilla gripped him tight, as if she were afraid her body would spin out of control if she weren't holding on.

His mouth on hers was a revelation. His lips were smooth and firm and his tongue plunged between her lips, demanding a response. She willingly gave it to him and he groaned, his grip on her tightening as their kiss burned out of control.

They'd kissed two other times and both those kisses had scoured through her like a forest fire, leaving her stunned and raw. But *this* kiss. Oh, this one had ten times the power of those. One hundred times the power.

Because she'd never quite felt this level of need for a man before. It was as if, now that she'd mentally surrendered to the moment, her body was playing catch-up on all the weeks of attraction she'd been suppressing.

She wanted to touch him everywhere, wanted to step inside his skin and be a part of him. His hands moved over her and then she was wedged tight against his body, her hips making contact with his hard thighs.

But there was more. His erection sizzled into her where it jutted insistently against her belly. Lucilla curved her hands around his buttocks and pulled him harder against her.

He made a sound in his throat that sent liquid heat coursing through her system. The robe was too confining, too hot, and she wanted it gone. But she couldn't take her hands off his body long enough to remove it.

Because touching him was amazing, thrilling. Now that she'd finally let herself go, kicked down the dam standing between her and this flood of sensation, she was overwhelmed. Her body ached and sizzled and hurt and she only wanted more of the same. No matter the consequences, she wanted more.

She wanted him everywhere. Right now.

She could feel the power in his body growing until suddenly he moved, hooking an arm behind her knees and sweeping her up. She didn't question him when he started walking toward her room.

He was through her door and to her bed in a few strides. And then he deposited her on her feet beside the bed. She clung to him, her arms wrapped around his powerful shoulders. She was taking such a risk, exposing herself to a maelstrom of dark, sensual feelings for this man she was at war with. But, right now, she didn't much care.

"You always wear your hair up," he said, his voice rough as he pulled her hair from the loose bun she'd wound it in for sleep. The elastic fell to the floor as her hair cascaded over her shoulders and Christos plunged his fingers into it. "I like it down."

"Then I'll keep wearing it up," she answered breathlessly, her pulse pounding in her temples, her throat, between her legs. She wanted him to kiss her again, right now, before she could think too hard, but he seemed content to run his hands through her hair.

"Because you like to do exactly the opposite of what I want? If I tell you I prefer you to keep your clothes on, will you take them off?"

A thrill shot through her. "I might."

His hands fell to her waist and he pulled her close.

"Then by all means, remain clothed, *glykia mou*. Do not kiss me. Do not touch me. Do not, under any circumstances, put your mouth anywhere on my body." His head dipped toward hers and her heart drummed a crazy beat. "Do not kiss me back, Lucilla…."

His mouth took hers then in a hot, wet, deep kiss that curled her toes and made her body sag in his arms. But she kissed him back. Of course she did. And she wrapped her arms around his neck, arching herself against him.

He shoved her robe from her body, slid his hands beneath the T-shirt she'd worn to sleep in. His hands on her skin were such sweet torture. His fingers glided over her flesh, his thumbs grazing over her nipples as she gasped. And then he jerked her T-shirt up and over her head, his mouth leaving hers for only a moment.

Cool air wafted over her bare skin. Her nipples beaded tight, aching for his touch…and then he touched them again, his thumbs flicking the hard nubs as she made a noise in her throat. Lucilla responded by shoving his briefs down his thighs.

When she curled her hand around him, he groaned. "*Glykia mou,* not too much of that."

It thrilled her to hear the need in his voice, the desperation, the control pushed almost to the breaking point. A shiver rolled through her as she gripped him tighter and slid her hand up and down his length.

"Lucilla…" His mouth moved down her throat, over her collarbone—and then he took one tight nipple in his mouth and sucked hard while she arched her back and cried out. She put her hands on his shoulders for balance. If he kept doing that, oh…

"You have the most beautiful breasts, so responsive. So perfect."

"Christos, please…I can't…" Every tug of his mouth on her breast sent a sweet spike of pleasure into her sex. Her clitoris throbbed with need. Her body was wet, ready, electric with the pain of wanting.

He slid her panties down her thighs and dropped them on the floor. And then he was pushing her back on the bed, hovering over her, his chest rising and falling as quickly as hers as he held himself above her.

She loved that he seemed to be as affected by this heat between them as she did. His eyes bored into her, stripping her to the bone. There were no secrets here, no plots or schemes or enemies. There was only flesh and blood and heat. Two people who desperately wanted something from each other.

Or did he? Was she just another conquest? Was he managing her, the same as he'd managed her siblings? Was that what this was about?

She couldn't think that way. Lucilla pushed him over until he was on his back and she was on top. It was dark, but not so dark she couldn't see the outlines of his body. And of course he was beautiful. His penis stood tall and proud and she took him in hand again. Then she bent and licked him and he stiffened beneath her touch.

"Definitely don't do that," he growled.

"Oh, no, I won't…"

She took him in her mouth then, enjoyed the way he groaned, the way he gasped her name. She'd never yet had Christos at her mercy, but this was almost too much. He was hers to control so long as she had him in her mouth. Satisfaction flared inside her as her tongue glided over him again and again.

He was beautifully made, exciting, and she wanted more. She wanted to prove her mastery over him suddenly, wanted him to come, his body wild and out of control as he jerked and gasped his pleasure.

But Christos was not so far gone that he couldn't find the strength of will to drag her up and into his arms. He kissed her, turning her over until he was between her legs.

"Please tell me you are prepared, *glykia mou*. I did not come over here for sex, no matter what you might think when I arrived with dinner."

"In the drawer," she said, thankful she kept condoms there even though she hadn't had a love life in so long it seemed a bit desperate to do so. Somehow he found them in the dark. She took the packet from him, tearing it and throwing it on the floor as she grabbed him and rolled on the condom. He growled while she smoothed it on— and then she felt him, big and hard and right there—

"Oh, God," she gasped as he slid inside her, stretching her wide.

Christos stilled. "Second thoughts, Lucilla? Because this isn't a good time for them." He dragged in a ragged breath. "And yet I will stop if it's what you want."

She tightened her arms around him. "No, don't stop. It's just… It's been a while."

She hated to admit that, and yet she wasn't so prideful as to keep it a secret when it could physically hurt her not to tell him the truth.

He kissed her softly. "Then I promise to make it good for you." His hand slid between their bodies, found the hidden pearl of her sex. Sensation streaked through her as he moved his thumb over the tiny bundle of nerves again and again.

Soon she was arching her hips against him, seeking the next level of pleasure. He took her all the way to the edge—and then let her tumble over. Lucilla's body splintered apart as she cried out. And still he was deep inside her, hard and unmoving. Waiting.

When the tremors subsided, a thread of panic began to unwind inside her. What was she doing? What was she thinking to be having sex with Christos? *Sex with Christos!*

"Lucilla," he said. "Come back to me. I need you with me."

She swallowed. "I'm here."

"Are you? Or are you thinking this is a mistake?"

"I don't know—"

He moved his hips and fire streaked through her, silencing her as she tried to find her voice again. "How can this be anything but right?" he whispered. "Anything but precisely what was meant to happen from the first moment we met?"

"I don't know," she said on a choked whisper. Because, with just that little movement of his body, she wanted him more than ever. She wanted to immolate herself in his fire until there was nothing left but ashes.

"Brace yourself, *glykia mou,* because I intend to prove it to you."

His mouth captured hers almost savagely—and then he began to move. Soon, his body set up a rhythm she couldn't ignore, thrusting hard into her, drawing her deeper into this ocean of pleasure that existed between them. He dropped his head to her breasts, sucked her aching nipples. Lucilla's body sparked again, until she was on fire, until sensation rioted beneath her skin, dancing on millions of tiny nerve endings. Until she thought she would explode if she didn't reach the peak soon.

Pleasure dipped and rose and carried her on waves of fire, her core tightening as Christos moved again and again. And then it happened, that moment when every sensation converged inside her, imploding until she could see nothing but white behind her eyes, hear nothing but her heartbeat, feel nothing but the pleasure radiating outward, sparkling and snapping and making her sob his name.

"Yes," he said, his voice harsh in her ear. "Yes, like *that*."

And then he followed her into the abyss, her name a broken groan on his lips.

CHAPTER SEVEN

LUCILLA WOKE ALONE. The pale light of dawn slanted through the curtains and drifted across the tangle of covers on her bed. She lay there quietly, listening for Christos. There was no movement she could hear, so she got up and put on her robe before padding into the living room. The lights were on again, but the apartment was empty.

She checked the guest room, her heart beating a little faster with every step she took.

Empty.

He'd left. She stood there in stunned silence as she processed it all. Her body was still sore with the evidence of his possession and he'd walked out while she slept. Without saying goodbye. Without even a thank-you-for-the-sex-and-see-you-around.

You chose this, she told herself. *This is what happens when you let go.*

Yes, she'd finally let go. She'd stopped holding back and she'd taken what she wanted—repeatedly—until they were both exhausted. They'd collapsed together, lying in each other's arms, and drifted off to sleep.

She'd thought he would be here this morning, but perhaps it was a good thing he wasn't. Lucilla sniffed.

Yes, that was right. It was a *good* thing he wasn't. They weren't lovers, this wasn't an affair and it was better this way. Less messy.

They'd had a one-off. Because he was sexy and she was lonely and the timing had just worked out.

It didn't mean there would be anything more. Or that she wanted there to be.

No, she didn't *want* more of Christos. She'd had her fill. He was a dynamic lover, but she was done. Her body was satiated and she could get on with business now.

Lucilla showered and dressed carefully—sky-high leopard-print heels, a black pencil skirt and a white button-down shirt. She added a wide belt and checked her reflection. She remembered him saying he liked her hair down, his gravelly voice reaching deep inside her and making her feel beautiful and desirable, so she ruthlessly wrapped her hair up into a bun. She didn't want Christos to think for one moment she'd left it down for him.

When she was satisfied, she grabbed a banana from the kitchen—ignoring the Greek leftovers in the fridge that somehow made her heart clench when she got the milk for her coffee—and went to hail a taxi. She arrived at the hotel by eight, smiling and chatting with everyone as she worked her way toward her office.

Her heart beat hard as she passed Christos's office. Was he there? Was he thinking about her at all? Or had he completely moved on from last night? Her stomach twisted. That was the worst thought of all—that she'd been nothing more than an opportunity. That he'd used her body for his pleasure and left because he was finished.

Which, she had to admit, was the most likely scenario. Not that it mattered. She'd used him, too. She'd been thinking about buying a vibrator in the moments before she'd gone to knock on his door, for heaven's sake. He'd simply been a means to an end—and more convenient at that precise moment.

Lucilla sat down at her desk and called up her email. She had several to go through and a busy morning ahead. There was a wedding party this coming weekend, a corporate function on Monday and, of course, she had the shareholders' meeting—and the trip afterward—to prepare for.

A message arrived in her in-box.

Sara@Norringtons.co.uk
To: Lucilla.Chatsfield@TheChatsfield.com
Subject: PRIVATE
Found him.
S.N.

Her heart turned over. She sat there and stared at the email, feeling both an overwhelming curiosity and a biting guilt at the same time. She thought of Christos as he'd looked last night when he answered the bedroom door—rumpled, wild and completely vulnerable in a way she hadn't expected.

And then she thought of the way he'd turned her world upside down for a few hours of bliss. Lucilla closed her eyes and swallowed. Just thinking of the two of them in bed together made the temperature in the room rise. She had an urge to unbutton her shirt and fan herself.

Her office phone buzzed, making her jump. She hit the button. "Yes?"

"Mr. Giatrakos wishes to see you in his office," Jessie said.

A thread of panic unwound in her belly. He was summoning her after everything that had happened last night? She couldn't quite bear the thought. How was she supposed to walk into his office and pretend everything was normal?

"Tell him I'm busy."

"Yes, Ms. Chatsfield."

She turned back to her computer, determined to get through her email. The message from Sara was seared into her brain, but she suddenly didn't want to know what the other woman had found.

Which was completely ridiculous and made her precisely the sort of person Christos thought she was—indecisive and unwilling to make the hard choices. Finally, she snatched her phone up and hit the contact list so she could call Sara.

Her door burst open and she dropped the phone onto her desk. Christos stood there, looking cool and handsome in a black tailored suit that fit him like a glove. His shirt was sky-blue today, like his eyes, and the effect was nothing short of spectacular.

Her heart thudded. Moisture pooled between her legs. Oh, bloody hell…

"May I help you, Mr. Giatrakos?" She tried so hard to be cool and impersonal, but she could feel the tiny waver in her voice.

Christos's eyes narrowed. He closed the door firmly and ranged toward her, a sleek panther on the prowl. "You did not come when I sent for you."

She leaned back in her chair and tried not to let the tremor shimmering over her entire body show. "Clearly, there was no need. You came to me."

He studied her as if she were a newly discovered species. "Are you avoiding me, Ms. Chatsfield?"

"Not at all." She gestured toward her computer. "I am busy, as you can see. I can't drop everything I'm doing just to come and bow in your presence."

"You work here. When I need to speak to you, I need to speak to you. Did you consider it might be important?"

"Your summons did not mention importance."

He stopped in front of her desk, looking down at her so intensely that she wanted to tear her gaze away from his. She did not, though it was damned difficult. It was her office, her desk, her space—and yet he made her feel like she was the supplicant.

"You are angry with me."

Her stomach bottomed out. He was going there. She didn't want to talk about it, but he was going there, anyway. "Why would I be?"

"Because I wasn't there when you woke."

She shrugged as if she couldn't care less. "We had sex, Christos. I didn't require warm cuddles afterward. You were gone. Big deal."

She thought he looked surprised but then he masked it. "You are most reasonable for a woman," he said softly, and irritation sizzled into her. As if he were a great prize that women simply couldn't get enough of.

She picked up a pen and slid it between her fingers just to have something to do. "What did you expect? Did you want me to beg you for another night in your arms? Did you think you'd find me weepy and clingy and inconsolable because you left while I was asleep?" She shook her head. "I was relieved you were gone. It saved me the trouble of asking you to go."

His eyes had narrowed again. She couldn't tell what was happening in that brain of his, but she'd wager at least part of it was shock. Satisfaction swelled in her veins. *Take that, Mr. Sexy Greek*.

"Then it is a relief for us both," he said, his voice somewhere between a purr and a growl.

She tried not to let his words prick her, but they did, anyway. She knew what kind of man he was. And she'd slept with him regardless. Well, then. They'd had sex. Wonderful, incredible, mind-blowing sex—at least for her—and it was over.

She should be relieved. She wasn't.

"Of course it is," she lied. "Now what did you need? I have a lot to do before next week if I'm to accompany you on this tour. Or did you come to tell me I'm not needed now?"

Part of her hoped he would say that, and part of her thought she might scream if he did. She wanted to tour the other hotels and, oddly enough, she wanted him to treat her like she was a valuable asset to the Chatsfield empire.

"You will still accompany me. And what I wanted from you, Ms. Chatsfield, was a summary report of your department's performance for the past month. You do remember those, yes?"

A blush heated her skin. Dammit. "Of course I do. You only sent about a hundred memos regarding monthly reports."

"And yet you are late with yours. The only department head who is, I might add."

Anger simmered just beneath the surface. "Then perhaps you should get out of my office so I can finish the report." She smiled politely, but if he looked closely enough he'd see the steel behind it. And the utter fury.

"On my desk by noon, Ms. Chatsfield," he said as he walked to the door.

"As you command, O Supreme Overlord," she replied, still smiling. With one last swift look she couldn't decipher, he walked out and shut the door behind him. Lucilla hurled the pen. It hit the door with a thunk.

Then she snatched up her phone and dialed Sara Norrington.

Christos returned to his office and slammed the door harder than he intended. No doubt Sophie was cringing at her desk in response but he could not find it in himself to reassure her. He stormed over to the window and stared out at the park across the street, his gut churning with anger and frustration.

And thwarted need. That was the most puzzling of all. He'd had Lucilla Chatsfield last night—more than once—but he wanted more. He wasn't done with her, and that was most unusual. And alarming.

He did not emotionally attach himself to anyone. He'd learned a long time ago that caring for another person made you vulnerable in the most horrific ways imaginable. He'd loved one person in his life, and he'd nearly sacrificed his entire future for her. When he thought of his mother's face—her beautiful, battered face, shining with tears—and the sheer rage that had welled up in him that night when his father had come home drunk and angry and intent on hitting something, he remembered why he did not allow himself to feel anything for anyone.

Not that a single night in Lucilla's bed meant he felt something. Far from it. He'd awakened around four this

OFFICIAL OPINION POLL

Dear Reader,

Since you are a book enthusiast, we would like to know what you think.

Inside you will find a short Opinion Poll. Please participate in our poll by sharing your opinion on 3 subjects that are very important to all of us.

To thank you for your participation, we would like to send you **2 FREE BOOKS** and **2 FREE GIFTS!**

Please enjoy them with our compliments.

Sincerely,

Pam Powers

YOUR OPINION POLL
THANK-YOU FREE GIFTS INCLUDE:

▶ **2 FREE BOOKS**

▶ **2 LOVELY SURPRISE GIFTS**

OFFICIAL OPINION POLL

YOUR OPINION COUNTS!
Please check TRUE or FALSE below to express your opinion about the following statements:

Q1 Do you believe in "true love"?

"TRUE LOVE HAPPENS ONLY ONCE IN A LIFETIME."
○ TRUE
○ FALSE

Q2 Do you think marriage has any value in today's world?

"YOU CAN BE TOTALLY COMMITTED TO SOMEONE WITHOUT BEING MARRIED."
○ TRUE
○ FALSE

Q3 What kind of books do you enjoy?

"A GREAT NOVEL MUST HAVE A HAPPY ENDING."
○ TRUE
○ FALSE

YES! I have placed my sticker in the space provided below. Please send me the **2 FREE** books and **2 FREE gifts** for which I qualify. I understand that I am under no obligation to purchase anything further, as explained on the back of this card.

❑ I prefer the regular-print edition
106/306 HDL GGEL

❑ I prefer the larger-print edition
176/376 HDL GGEL

FIRST NAME

LAST NAME

ADDRESS

APT.#

CITY

STATE/PROV.

ZIP/POSTAL CODE

HP-N14-TF-13

HARLEQUIN™ READER SERVICE —Here's How It Works:

Accepting your 2 free Harlequin Presents® books and 2 free gifts (gifts valued at approximately $10.00) places you under no obligation to buy anything. You may keep the books and gifts and return the shipping statement marked "cancel." If you do not cancel, about a month later we'll send you 6 additional books and bill you just $4.30 each for the regular-print edition or $5.05 each for the larger-print edition in the U.S. or $4.99 each for the regular-print edition or $5.49 each for the larger-print edition in Canada. That is a savings of at least 14% off the cover price. It's quite a bargain! Shipping and handling is just 50¢ per book in the U.S. and 75¢ per book in Canada.* You may cancel at any time, but if you choose to continue, every month we'll send you 6 more books, which you may either purchase at the discount price or return to us and cancel your subscription. *Terms and prices subject to change without notice. Prices do not include applicable taxes. Sales tax applicable in N.Y. Canadian residents will be charged applicable taxes. Offer not valid in Quebec. Books received may not be as shown. All orders subject to credit approval. Credit or debit balances in a customer's account(s) may be offset by any other outstanding balance owed by or to the customer. Please allow 4 to 6 weeks for delivery. Offer available while quantities last.

BUSINESS REPLY MAIL
FIRST-CLASS MAIL   PERMIT NO. 717   BUFFALO, NY

POSTAGE WILL BE PAID BY ADDRESSEE

HARLEQUIN READER SERVICE
PO BOX 1867
BUFFALO NY 14240-9952

NO POSTAGE
NECESSARY
IF MAILED
IN THE
UNITED STATES

If offer card is missing write to: Harlequin Reader Service, P.O. Box 1867, Buffalo NY 14240-1867 or visit www.ReaderService.com

morning. It had taken him a few moments to recall where he was and who he was with. She'd been curled into his side, an arm thrown possessively over his waist, and he'd lain there thinking back on everything that had happened between them.

He was a man who enjoyed sex and a variety of partners. He'd had partners who were more adventurous and skilled, certainly. But at that moment he'd only wanted to wake her up and do everything again.

It was a novel feeling. He did not enjoy novel feelings. They were outside of his comfort zone, so he'd eased himself from the bed and gone back to the guest room. There, he'd dressed in the dark, intent on leaving before she woke.

But he'd not been able to leave without going back into the bedroom and looking at her one last time. Her body was lush under the sheet and her mouth was slack with sleep. Her hair was a tangle of chestnut and he'd found himself reaching out to smooth it along the pillow.

Why?

He did not know, but he'd straightened and then turned and walked out without another glance. Lucilla Chatsfield was no different than any other woman. His fascination with her stemmed from her unwillingness to succumb to his charm the way other women did. He told himself on the taxi ride home that she would be a different woman today, that when he summoned her to his office she would come willingly—breathlessly— and he would be able to shut the door and take her in his arms if that's what he desired.

And then he'd decided he would *have* to make love to her again just to keep her pliable and cooperative while he reshaped the Chatsfield holdings and rehabilitated their reputation. It would not be a hardship to do so and when he was finished, when the work was done, he could let Lucilla down gently.

It had been the perfect plan. Until she'd refused his summons. Until she'd sat at her desk, looked at him all cool and businesslike and told him she was grateful he'd left so she wouldn't have to ask him to leave. He'd felt as if he'd landed in an alternate reality in which the tables were turned and he was the supplicant.

He did not like it. Not one bit.

Christos raked a hand through his hair and then went to fling himself in his chair. Lucilla was nothing to him. Nothing whatsoever. If she wanted to pretend they'd never been lovers, he was fine with it. More than fine. So long as she did her job, he didn't care what she did on her off time—or whom she did it with.

Yet he remembered her telling him last night, with that breathless little hitch in her voice, that it had been a long time since she'd had sex. He'd felt the tension in her body, the tremors that shook her, and he'd experienced a rush of tenderness for her in that moment.

He was her first in a long time. It was a crime since she was so beautiful, but after working with her for the past couple of months, he knew why she didn't take lovers. She was too uptight, too focused on the work.

Well, so was he. He had a job to do here and that was the most important thing. It had always been the most important thing. He'd vowed in the juvenile-detention center that he would never allow himself to react emotionally again. He'd had to fight almost daily at first to establish his dominance, but once he had he'd turned to the library and read every last book they had.

When more books came, he read those, too. When

he was released at eighteen, he'd changed everything about himself—his name, his accent, his manners, his education—and become someone new. There was no reason to remain the person he'd been. His mother was dead and his father was a bastard who would never again mess with the son he'd beaten senseless more than once.

From that day forward, Christos had been a new man. He never looked back.

He rubbed a hand over his temple as he read through the reports on his computer screen. Yes, he dreamed sometimes. He could still taste the fear and rage he'd felt that night in his parents' home, and all the other nights when his brute of a father had come back after falling off the wagon and carousing in bars. The life they'd led had been good for long stretches of time, punctuated by bouts of hell. It was the hell that had shaped him into the man he'd become.

And it was that hell he couldn't quite forget, no matter how successful he became or how far behind he left the angry, abused boy he'd been. That boy still came to him in dreams, and no matter how Christos tried to tell him it would be okay, the boy didn't know it. He was scared and angry and he did things he shouldn't do.

The intercom buzzed and he punched the button impatiently. "What is it?"

Sophie's voice was professionally detached, but he knew she wasn't particularly a fan of his. Not after he'd sent her to secure Nicolo Chatsfield's attendance at the shareholders' meeting. She'd come back a different woman than when she'd left. But she'd accomplished the impossible and that's all he cared about.

The impossible was his specialty, after all.

"It's Ms. Chatsfield, sir. She's here to see you."

Christos didn't like the little stab of excitement that speared into him at the thought. "Send her in."

"Yes, sir."

The door opened and Lucilla stood there, remote and beautiful. He had to swallow his tongue because he hadn't seen what she was wearing when she sat behind her desk. The black skirt and white shirt were expected, but the leopard-print heels were not. Her legs were a mile long in those things—and he had a sudden memory of them wrapped around his waist while he pounded into her.

"What is it, Ms. Chatsfield?" he said, feigning boredom. He couldn't stand, however, or she'd see he was anything but. His body was hardening by degrees as he looked at her standing there like a conquering Amazon.

She shut the door firmly behind her and came over to stand in front of his desk. He sprawled lazily, his suit jacket at least hiding the evidence of his attraction to her.

"I want you to go," she said softly. The gold flecks in her eyes sparked, but not in passion. Anger, no doubt. Except her tone was not angry at all. It was…resigned, he thought.

"That's not a secret, Lucilla *mou*."

"I mean it, Christos. This time, you're leaving. Call my father and give your notice. And then get the hell out of my company and my life."

A prickle of alarm slid along the back of his neck, raising the hairs there. He let his chair rock forward very slowly. And then he stood. They faced each other across the desk and he noticed that her chin trembled. Just once. Just barely.

So strong, this woman. So repressed.

"I'm afraid I can't do that, darling. I don't walk away

until the job is done. And it's not. I'm sorry if you've decided to have an attack of conscience over last night, but it changes nothing. I'm here to stay."

Her eyes held his and her chin lifted. He pictured Boudicca rousing the tribes against the Romans.

"You need to rethink your answer. Or you can tell the shareholders in just a few days precisely who Nikos Stavrou is."

Ice formed into a ball in his belly. But he would not react. "And who do you think he is?" he asked mildly. Dangerously.

She swallowed. "I know who he is," she said. "He's a criminal. And he's you."

CHAPTER EIGHT

LUCILLA COULD NOT believe what she'd just been told. Her stomach roiled in fury and pain. The triumph she'd expected to feel was strangely absent. She'd wanted to find out something about Christos, something to make him go away—but she hadn't expected this.

He stood there so tall and remote and angry, his eyes flashing hot. He was not in the least bit cowed—and had she really expected he would be?

"I don't know what you think you know about me, Lucilla *mou,* but there is nothing you can say that will make me quit."

She sucked in a pained breath. He'd been in her bed last night. He'd been a tender and amazing lover, both giving and demanding. He'd coaxed responses from her body that had stunned her. Responses she wanted to experience again and again.

But he wasn't who she thought he was. He was not the cool, urbane man of mystery he pretended to be. He was a violent criminal. Or had been.

"You nearly killed a man," she said, her throat tight. "Your own father."

His face morphed into a cold mask. His eyes gave nothing away. They were curiously blank, and somehow that hurt far more than if he'd stayed angry or become suddenly remorseful. If he'd broken down and said how he'd made a youthful mistake, how he regretted his actions, how he'd built himself into a better man because he knew he'd needed to do so, then she might have felt a wave of sympathy for him.

As it was, she felt angry, betrayed—and sad. So very sad. Who was this man she'd given herself to last night? She couldn't forget the way he'd looked when he'd opened the guest-room door—lost and alone and almost terrified—but how did that mesh with who she now knew him to be?

"I did indeed," he said, his voice cold and empty. "And I served my time for it, too."

She wrapped her arms around herself. "Yet you keep it hidden. And you changed your name."

A flash of anger did cross his features then. "Of course I did. I was a child, Lucilla, and I made a mistake. Is that supposed to follow me for the rest of my life?"

"But your father…" She felt many things for her own father, but not the kind of hate that could make her want to kill him. Never that. Disappointment and love and exasperation, yes.

His jaw was tight. "Just because a man makes a baby with a woman doesn't mean he's a father."

"It also doesn't mean he deserves what you did to yours." Her voice was barely more than a whisper. It hurt to say such things to him, and yet she couldn't understand how he could have done what the detective told her.

Nikos Stavrou spent four years in a juvenile-detention facility for attacking his father and nearly killing the man. No, the Stavrou home was not a happy one. The father was drunk and disorderly much of the time, and the police were often called out for domestic disturbances. But to attack your own father with a club and beat him so badly he spent two months in the hospital and now lived on disability?

It made her shudder to think the same man who had done those things had touched her so tenderly last night. He'd stroked her skin like she was a cherished possession, but those same hands had wielded a weapon against his own father.

"I won't discuss this with you, Lucilla. It's none of your goddamned business."

The lump in her throat was huge. She didn't understand, and yet she also felt as if she'd crossed some sort of line she shouldn't by bringing this up. But what choice did she have? He couldn't stay. She couldn't allow a man like him to run this company and sit in judgment of her and her family when he had no right to be so judgmental.

"No, it's not," she said. "But the Chatsfield is. And I want you gone. Give your notice, Christos. Call my father and make it happen."

His eyes glittered dangerously. For someone who should be intimidated right now, he certainly wasn't showing any signs of it. "I'm not afraid of you, Lucilla."

"I'm giving you until the shareholders' meeting. If you aren't gone by then, I'll have a lot to say when it's my turn to speak."

"What a cold bitch you are," he said softly, and she felt the blow of those words like he'd stabbed her in the heart. "So superior and morally indignant. But don't forget when you're looking down your spoiled nose at me that I know what kind of sounds you make when you come. I've heard you beg, Lucilla. For me. For *my* touch."

She swallowed. "That's before I knew—"

"You'd beg me again, right now, right here, if I kissed you. You'd beg me, Lucilla. Don't ever forget that."

She backed up instinctively, her heart thumping in her breast. Because if he came around that desk and took her in his arms, she was afraid he might prove his point. Because part of her ached for him. Part of her remembered that wild, lonely man and the refuge they'd found together in her bed. For a few hours, neither of them had been alone.

An illusion, she told herself. Christos was never alone because women fell at his feet all the time. She, however, had made their night into something more without intending to. She'd actually started to like him, just a teeny bit. But it was false. He wasn't even who he said he was, so how much of a stretch was it for him to pretend last night? Pretend that what they'd shared had been important, at least for that bit of time they were together?

"The meeting, Christos," she said as she reached the door. "Give your notice and you can address the meeting as if everything is normal. Say you got another offer. I don't care. But do it or so help me…"

She couldn't look at his face a moment longer, couldn't see the rage and frustration—and regret?—playing across his features without wanting to rush to his side and put her arms around him.

She reached for the door blindly, found it and yanked it open. She was back inside her office, trembling and gulping air, when she realized that tears dripped from her cheeks. It had been so long since she'd cried. So damn long.

But she couldn't hold it back another moment. She sank into a chair and put her face in her hands. Then she sobbed.

Lucilla's phone rang that night, startling her out of a half sleep. She was still on her sofa, papers arrayed before her. She'd had a hard time concentrating on them as guilt and anger vied for dominance.

She found her phone beneath a pile of papers. It was Christos's number and her heart dropped before soaring inexplicably.

"Yes?" she said, her voice scratchy and uncertain. She closed her eyes and prayed for composure.

"I want to talk to you."

"You *are* talking to me."

"In person, Lucilla."

"I'll be in at eight in the morning."

"Now."

She shoved her hair back from her face. "Then talk on the phone. It's all you're getting."

He blew out a breath. "Very well. I want to know how you learned this information."

Her heart ached. "I hired someone."

"Clearly." He sounded so cold and she hated it. "It must have cost you a lot of money."

"I have money. You know it because my father put you in charge of the trust."

"Yes. I wonder that you did not buy your mother's portrait, but you spend a fortune to uncover my past. Do you hate me that much, Lucilla?"

Her heart throbbed at the reminder of her mother's picture. It had been a necessary sacrifice not to bid on it. But why did she now feel like the one who was wrong?

Why did she hurt for him? "I don't hate you," she said, and meant it for once. "I just want my rightful place in my own damn company."

"It's not yours," he said. "It's your father's. And your siblings'. It belongs to all of you. And I am the right person to return it to its glory days."

"I'm capable, Christos."

"You are. But you lack experience. I've turned around more companies before breakfast than you've ever even thought about. But you go ahead, Lucilla *mou,* do things your way."

Her breath caught. "You're resigning?"

"Does that make you happy?"

Yes. And no. Dammit! "Of course it does." She sucked in a deep breath. "I won't tell anyone, Christos. You have my word on that. Resign, and I'll tear up the report."

She thought he chuckled softly. "You drive a hard bargain, kitten. The Chatsfield is yours. Run it into the ground for all I care."

"I'm not trying to hurt you," she said softly.

"Hurt me?" He sounded surprised. "You can't, Lucilla. I'd have to care first."

He hung up then, and she just sat there with her phone to her ear, thinking how empty it made her feel not to hear him breathing.

Lucilla did not feel all that triumphant over the next few days as the shareholders' meeting approached. Christos looked through her most of the time. When he did look at her, there wasn't an ounce of feeling in his icy eyes. His gaze passed over her and she felt as if a winter storm had ravaged her every time.

She hadn't told anyone about the report. She'd even held off telling Antonio. She wasn't sure why, but she didn't want to share this information just yet. Besides, Antonio was still working on taking over the Kennedy hotels and she didn't want to distract him. Having those hotels added to the Chatsfield holdings would only cement her position as the rightful CEO once Christos was gone.

Once Christos was gone.

That thought didn't make her as happy as it once had, which made her furious with herself. Why was she so maudlin? Just because they'd slept together one stormy night? Because she'd seen him vulnerable and human? It wasn't enough, she reminded herself. If she let herself feel sorry for him, she was no better than he'd told her she was weeks ago. She'd been tough and ruthless, just like he'd told her she needed to be, so why was she always thinking about it?

She worked late on the night before the meeting, going over her business plan and spreadsheets. Once Christos left, her father might try to bring someone else in, but she wouldn't give him that opportunity. She would prove she was the logical successor, and she would do everything so perfectly that Gene Chatsfield could think of no one better to oversee the family business.

When she knew everything was perfect, she turned off her computer and checked her watch. It was just after eight in the evening. She yawned and stood, placing all her papers in her briefcase. Then she turned off her light and walked out. Christos's door was open and a light burned at his desk. She thought about sneaking past, but then she squared her shoulders and walked over to the threshold.

Christos looked up, his face startlingly handsome in the low light of a desk lamp. She'd kissed his firm jaw, thrust her tongue between his sensual lips. Felt his lips on her body. *Everywhere* on her body.

"Ah, Lucilla, come in." He stood and walked over to the liquor cabinet contained inside an antique Edwardian sideboard. "Have a drink with me."

"I shouldn't," she said as a wave of guilt rose inside her.

"Just one. A toast to the future. Your future."

She stepped inside his office almost reluctantly. "Maybe just one." How could she refuse when she was getting precisely what she wanted? She'd won. She'd rousted him from her company and this was the eve of her triumph.

He poured vodka in a glass and added tonic and a twist of lime. Then he held it out to her. "Your favorite, correct?"

It shocked her that he knew. "Yes."

Their fingers touched as she took it. Her skin burned from the contact but she did not snatch her hand away.

"I observe, Lucilla *mou*. You drink vodka and tonic, pinot grigio and cabernet sauvignon with the occasional malbec tossed in for variety. These are your drinks."

She set her case down on a chair. "They are." It embarrassed her that she did not know his. He'd had wine with her that night he'd brought dinner over—but she didn't know what he actually preferred.

He poured Scotch in a glass and she thought, *Aha*. And then she felt a twinge of sadness because why did it matter?

He held up his glass. "To you, Lucilla. You've won the battle."

"I'm sorry, Christos," she caught herself saying.

He shrugged and took a drink. Then he leaned against the cabinet and watched her. "Aren't you going to drink to your triumph?"

She didn't really have a taste for alcohol right this minute. Her stomach churned like she was a girl again. A girl who was filled with fear and worry for her family and who didn't know how to make things right. She'd tried, but it had cost her so much. Her dreams, her independence for a very long time, and even her health when she'd been diagnosed with an ulcer at the tender age of seventeen.

But that was a long time ago and she didn't have ulcers anymore. She lifted the glass and took a drink. The vodka burned going down and she nearly coughed. But she didn't. She swallowed hard and put the drink down on a table. Then she picked up her briefcase. The room seemed a little wobbly when she straightened again and she admonished herself. She really needed to eat better.

She couldn't exist on energy drinks and sugary pastries—with the occasional piece of fruit thrown in—if she were going to maintain her health and run this company properly.

"I'm sorry it had to be this way," she said—was she slurring? Lucilla blinked as the room seemed a little wobblier. Then she put her hand to her head.

Christos was at her side. "Why don't you sit a moment? You look green."

She felt green. He eased her into the chair and she sat there for a moment, feeling so sleepy that she wanted to put her head back on the soft cushions and take a nap. Christos was frowning down at her, his hands in his pockets now.

"I'm sorry," she said. "I'm just so tired."

"Then close your eyes and rest."

She forced her eyes open and tried to stand. "No, I should go home. Much to prepare for."

Christos's hand was on her shoulder, pushing her gently back into the chair. "Sleep, *glykia mou*. All will be well when you awake."

CHAPTER NINE

WHEN LUCILLA WOKE, she was in a bed. She lay there for a moment, her head fuzzy, and tried to remember how she'd gotten here. She'd been in her office, it had been late, and then she'd stopped for a drink with Christos. She didn't remember anything after that. She must have been so tired she'd taken a taxi home and collapsed in her bed.

She pushed herself up on an elbow, frowning as she did so. She would almost swear she could hear the ocean...

Which was insane. She did not hear the ocean. There was no ocean in London. She yawned and rubbed her hand over her face.

And then her heart began to race as she remembered what day this was. The shareholders' meeting! She had to get dressed and get to the office before it started. Christos would be announcing his departure and she would be there to step up to the plate and take responsibility for the future of the company.

She whipped the covers back and climbed from the bed—and then she stood there and wobbled for a moment. The room did not look familiar. In fact, it did not smell familiar. There was a hint of salt in the air. She wrinkled her nose—was that lemon?

The shutters were closed but light slanted in between them, making a grid on the floor. Shutters? She did not have shutters. Her heart skipping, Lucilla shuffled over to the nearest shutter and wrenched it wide.

The light was blinding and it took a few seconds of blinking before everything came into focus. She shook her head. Was she hallucinating? Everywhere she could see, there was nothing but blue. A large terrace gave way to an infinity pool and beyond that, stretching as far as the eye could see, was nothing but ocean. Her stomach fell to the floor as panic twisted itself into her brain.

Lucilla turned and ran over to the bedroom door. But when she tried to wrench it open, it didn't move. Fear crawled its way up her spine. But it didn't last long, because fury rode hard on its heels. She was not in England. She didn't know where she was, but someone had kidnapped her and whisked her away before the shareholders' meeting.

It had to be Christos, of course. No one else would do such a thing. But where had he sent her? And how in the hell was she going to escape and return to oust his sorry ass?

Lucilla turned and headed for the big glass windows that fronted the terrace. But they were locked, too. She considered picking up a chair and shattering the glass, but what good would it do if she cut herself in the process? Breaking windows wasn't nearly as easy as they made it look in the movies.

She spied a phone on the bedside table and wrenched up the receiver. There was no dial tone and she dropped it again with a frustrated growl.

Just then, the handle turned and she stood there with her heart in her throat as the door swung inward. She wasn't sure what she expected but the man standing there with a tray in his hands was certainly not it.

"Christos!"

He crossed the threshold. The smell of food made her stomach rumble but she was much too angry to eat.

"Good morning, Lucilla. I trust you slept well?"

She clenched her fists at her side. "Where am I? What have you done?"

He set the tray on the table at the foot of the bed and she decided not to wait for an answer. She rushed out the door and down a darkened stairwell until she burst into a spacious, light-filled living room that also looked out on the sea. On this side of the house, however, she could see a village and a harbor down below. The buildings were blinding white in the sun, the ocean so crystalline-blue and the surrounding land was clearly volcanic with raw cliff faces and smaller islands farther out to sea that were dotted with green.

She spun around to find Christos behind her, hands shoved in his pockets, watching her with those icy blue eyes that mirrored the color of the water. Confusion and pain slid into her.

"Greece?" she said. "You brought me to Greece."

He shrugged. "You left me no choice."

She shoved a hand through her hair. And then she caught her reflection in a mirror at the opposite end of the room. Her hair was a wild tangle of chestnut, her skin pale as cream and she was wearing a pair of panties and a touristy T-shirt that said I ♥ Kefalonia.

"I left you no choice? Christos, you kidnapped me!"

And then she realized how he must have done it. Her heart pounded in her chest. "My God, you drugged me."

"As I said, you left me no choice."

She shook her head violently. Tears sprang to her eyes. She'd wanted to believe in him. She *had* believed in him. Even though he'd done something terrible when he'd been a child, she'd told herself it was a long time ago. He was not a child anymore, and he was not violent.

But he was dishonest. And maybe he was still violent, too. How did she really know?

Fear uncoiled itself in her belly. Just as quickly, her heart said, *No*. He was not the kind of man who would hurt her. He'd been so wonderful, so tender, that night when they'd made love. And he didn't have to be. He could have taken her hard, violently, and walked away without another look. But he'd been gentle when she'd told him it had been a long time.

And he'd been lost when she'd knocked on the guest-room door. She couldn't forget that.

But this…this was beyond comprehension.

"I want to leave. Now."

"You may leave anytime you wish, Lucilla. But I'm asking you to stay."

She folded her arms around her body, feeling exposed and alone and confused. "Why would I do that? It's obvious I can't trust you. You've *abducted* me!"

He didn't look apologetic. "You threatened my entire career—not to mention the life I've carefully built in the wake of everything that nearly destroyed me."

"But I didn't. I said I wouldn't tell anyone. I promised to shred the report!"

It was his turn to look angry. "And I should believe you? You were willing to expose me to the shareholders of the Chatsfield if I did not do what you wanted. How do I know you won't come after me later, when you feel I've caused you some new slight?"

"I would never do such a thing." She spoke stiffly, but his laugh was bitter.

"Of course not. When I go to work for some other company, when that company ends up threatening yours, you will not use what you know to make me, once again, back off, no?" He moved closer to her, his big body vibrating with anger and indignation, and she felt chastised when she was supposed to be furious. "How could I let you possess such life-altering information without forcing you to confront the circumstances of my past? If you still wish to destroy me, then by all means. But you will *not* do it without knowing what it is you have chosen to destroy. You owe me that much."

"I owe you nothing." Her voice was a whisper. Just saying the words made her throat hurt. But why did she owe him? He'd done nothing for her. And he'd drugged her.

One dark eyebrow arched. "No? Have you not seen the size of my severance package, Lucilla *mou?* If I leave, as you so vibrantly wish me to do, the company owes me quite a lot. Not as much as if you were to fire me outright, but enough to make you feel the pinch. Stay with me here, do as I ask and I won't take a penny. This will be what you owe me, and you will have paid it in full."

She swallowed. She hadn't considered his severance package. And she should have. A mistake on her part, but then her father would not have promised him more than they could afford. Except it would mean they'd have to make sacrifices in other areas of the business for a while.

But if she stayed, if she did as he asked, she'd walk away owing him nothing. It was a small price to pay. And yet he'd abducted her. She couldn't forget that.

"Why did you not ask me this in London?" she said tightly. "Why did you feel the need to bring me here against my will?"

He looked at her as if she were too stupid to understand the bigger picture. And she almost felt she was. Her brain didn't work the way his did. She wasn't capable of so much…deception. In her world, people acted honorably.

"If I had proposed this to you in London, you would have laughed. You believed you held the ace and you would not have compromised."

"I did hold the ace. Clearly, or you would not have gone to such lengths."

His smile was grim. "*Touché, Lucilla.* You begin to understand how the game is played. Yes, you held the ace and you were not inclined to listen to anything I had to say."

She became aware, as his gaze dropped down over her body, that she was standing here in her underwear and a T-shirt with no bra. Her nipples, traitors that they were, pressed against the thin cotton. She tightened her grip on herself and stood there with as much grace as she could.

"You drugged me."

"I did. It is a harmless drug, only meant to make you sleep. Which you have done."

"You undressed me," she accused. "You could have done anything to me."

He looked disgusted and she felt a pinch in her heart. "First, I am not so desperate as to take advantage of drugged women—especially not women I've already had, and with their permission, I might add. And second, I did not undress you. The housekeeper did, with the help of her daughter."

Lucilla darted a gaze around the room, expecting people to appear at any minute while she stood here so exposed.

"They have gone home for the day. She only came to open the house up and help me with you."

She relaxed only marginally. "How long have I been here?"

"We arrived in the early hours of the morning. It is noon now."

"You've missed the shareholders' meeting."

He shrugged. "Rescheduled at the last moment, I am afraid. Inconvenient for everyone, but unavoidable. They will get over it."

"And where are we supposed to be?"

"On our tour, of course. We are viewing potential properties for new investment."

She glanced out the window at the harbor again. "Which island is this?"

"It's on your shirt, I believe."

"I thought you were from Athens."

"That was later. Before that, I was from Kefalonia. Which I would think you would know, considering you spent so much to find out."

She swallowed. "The report only told me what you did and that you went to juvenile detention for it."

"I see."

Her stomach rumbled and a wave of dizziness passed over her. She reached for the back of a chair to steady herself. Christos was looking at her with narrowed eyes.

"You need to eat." He came forward and took her arm. She tried to yank free from his grip but he only held her tighter. "Be a sensible girl and don't fight me, Lucilla."

He led her back upstairs to the bedroom and ushered her over to the table. She didn't want to do a damn thing he said, but she was very hungry. She lifted the lid on the plate to reveal eggs, toast and ham. Christos poured a cup of coffee from a silver pot and added cream. It ought to surprise her that he knew how she liked her coffee, but she found that it did not. He was, she'd realized, very observant.

"Will I fall asleep again if I drink this?" she flung at him when he set it in front of her.

"No."

She took the cup in her hands and lifted the fragrant brew to her nose. It smelled right. "You'll understand if I don't quite believe you. This is my first abduction, after all."

"Mine, too," he said, and she almost wanted to laugh at the way he said it. But she didn't.

"Why was the door locked?"

"Because I didn't want you wandering outside before I had a chance to talk to you. It won't be locked again."

"The phone doesn't work."

"Not at all."

"Where's my mobile?"

"I have it."

"I want it back.

"Eat, Lucilla. Think about my proposal. You can have your phone back when you've given me an answer."

"And if the answer is no?"

He arched an eyebrow. "Then get prepared to open

up the bank vaults, *glykia mou*. Because I will demand my full severance."

"I could just threaten to release the information I have."

"You could. But that wouldn't stop you from owing me a severance package. Destroy me, and I'll respond in kind." He waved a hand at the view out the windows. "Eat. Enjoy. Come and see me when you've considered your options."

He turned and walked out and she sat there staring at the door he'd left wide open. Then she dug into the food and ate like she was starving.

Christos was not especially happy with himself at the moment. He stood on the terrace, gazing at the sea below, and feeling as if someone had turned him inside out. He did not often return to Kefalonia, though he'd bought this house here as a reminder of all that he'd achieved. The fisherman's son was now rich enough to buy his own island if he wanted it, but he remembered happier days here when he was little. Before his father had moved him and his mother to Athens and tried to find different work.

He'd spent years not caring what anyone thought of him, years keeping his soul very carefully guarded from any who sought to get close. Not that Lucilla had tried to get close to him, but something had happened that night in her apartment. Something very out of the ordinary. He wasn't in love, certainly not, but he was drawn to her in ways he'd never been drawn to another person.

And that had made him act in ways that were utterly uncharacteristic and somehow still shocking at the same time. No, he'd never abducted a soul—but there weren't many avenues of action he'd closed himself off from in his determination to win, other than illegal ones, of course.

He might be ruthless, but he'd only once reacted out of emotion instead of careful consideration. That had cost him four years of his life in which he'd vowed to never let emotion get the best of him ever again.

"I accept your proposition."

He turned and found Lucilla in the entry to the terrace, her long hair damp and hanging down her back, her face scrubbed free of all makeup—and somehow so breathtakingly innocent because of it. She was wearing a pair of jeans and a silky tank from the collection of clothing he'd had sent over from Athens. They fit her perfectly.

"I am glad to hear it."

She shrugged as she came out to join him. "I didn't think I had much choice, really. It costs me nothing to let you show me what you wish to show me. But you *are* still leaving the Chatsfield, Christos."

"As you wish."

She stepped up to him then, and before he could determine what she intended, she lashed out and slapped him across the face. Hard.

His head snapped back, his cheek stinging. He clenched his fists at his sides. The one thing he would never do was hit a woman, no matter the inducement. And yet no one had hit him in many years now. It was shocking to feel the weight of a blow on his flesh once more.

"That's for drugging me." Her eyes flashed hot, the golden flecks in them deepening to amber. "How dare you think that was okay?"

He reacted to the emotions boiling from her—and inside him, if he were to admit it—and yanked her into his arms. Then he crushed her mouth beneath his, punishing her with his kiss. Except who was he really punishing, he wondered, as the feel of her mouth against his sent a lightning bolt of longing straight down his spine and into his cock.

He held her tightly and kissed her hard, so hard his heart hammered in his chest and his brain began to beat the refrain that he had to stop or lose control. She wasn't pushing him away, surprisingly—her fists wrapped into his shirt and pulled him closer, as if she, too, couldn't get enough of this melding of mouths.

Somehow he found the strength to end the kiss, before he went beyond the boundaries of control. Before he shoved her down on the floor and took her hard and fast.

He shoved her away and she let him go as if burned. Her color was high, her lips bruised and reddened and slick. Her eyes flashed with desire and confusion. And then she brought the back of her hand up and very deliberately wiped her mouth, as if she were wiping away any trace of their kiss. As if it had been repellant to her.

"That," he said, his voice hard and low, "was for slapping me."

She stood there breathing hard for a moment. And then she stepped away from him as if nothing had happened.

"Well, now that we've got that out of the way." Her voice was light, breezy, but there was also a tremor in it and a red-hot bolt of possessiveness shot through him to know she was not unaffected. She walked over to the edge of the infinity pool and gazed beyond it to the sea and harbor below. "Thank you for the clothing," she said over her shoulder. "I'm no longer surprised that you seem to know my tastes in anything. Or, apparently, my size."

"I pay attention to details, Lucilla. Nothing more."

She spun to look at him, her eyes flashing with something other than anger this time. Hurt, maybe? Confusion? She masked it, however. "Well, you are very good indeed. I couldn't say what you like to eat or drink, or what size shoe you wear, if my life depended on it."

"Then you don't pay much attention to details, do you? You had dinner with me once. You must know what I ate that night."

Her cheeks glowed and he knew she was remembering more than the food. "Yes, I know that much. One meal, at least."

"Tonight you will know another. And if you wish to know my shoe size, you only need ask."

"I can't see why I need to know."

He shrugged. "You brought it up, not I."

"I was trying to prove a point."

"You do know things about me, Lucilla. Far more personal things than shoe size." He watched her chin lift, watched as the breeze off the sea blew a lock of hair across her face. She raked it back, but she didn't look at him.

"As you are so fond of saying, I had no choice. I will do whatever it takes to protect my legacy, Christos."

He almost laughed. "And I was not talking about the report."

CHAPTER TEN

SHE WAS ACUTELY aware of how her heart thumped against her chest, of the inexorable slide of her blood through her veins and of the throbbing response in her sex as his voice stroked over her nerve endings. Yes, she knew personal things about him that had nothing to do with the report.

His taste. His touch. The sounds he made when she took him in her mouth and pleasured him. The way he gasped her name in her ear, his breath hot and moist, as he pumped his seed into her. She knew his scents, his texture, his taste—and she could think of nothing else now that he'd reminded her.

"That was a mistake," she said, her throat tight. She couldn't forget that he'd nearly killed a man. And that he'd drugged her and hauled her to Greece while she couldn't protest. He'd taken away her choice, and she was furious with him.

"Perhaps, but nevertheless. It was a mistake you felt no compunction in repeating several times that night." His gaze stripped her bare in a way that she was learning only he could. "You know what it feels like to have me inside you, to scream my name when you come and to beg me for more. You enjoyed it, *glykia mou*. Do not pretend otherwise."

"It was just sex," she said. "It means nothing."

He arched an eyebrow. "Of this I am aware. But I will not let you lie to yourself about what happened. Sex, yes. But repeatedly, and with as much heat and ecstasy as I promised you that first night in your office."

She swallowed. Oh, yes, there had been heat and ecstasy aplenty. And, dammit, she would kill for more of the same. Even now her body was languid from his kiss. Aching, wanting. Her lips stung with the force of that kiss, but she knew his did, too. It would be impossible not to. She'd never kissed anyone with that much anger and violence boiling beneath the surface before. It almost frightened her. It most certainly intrigued her.

She wanted more. *No.*

Before she could frame a suitably nonchalant reply, he walked past her and into the house. She watched him go over to a desk, open it and pull something out. Then he came back and held it out to her.

"Your phone."

She took it, starting when his fingers brushed over hers. She hadn't really thought he would give it back so easily and she clutched the phone in her fingers as another feeling moved through her: confusion.

"I'm surprised you trust me enough to return it."

"I trust no one, Lucilla. But you will not go back on your word."

"And what if I lied just to get my phone back? I could call for help."

His eyes gleamed. "You could. But I think you're smarter than that. You care too much about your empire to risk any of its capital when you have a far easier way out. Though it may rankle you to stay, you will do so."

She didn't want to respect that brain of his, or to agree with his assessment. But she did. She usually did, damn him.

"I will," she said. "Now what am I here for?"

Because she wanted it done and over before these chaotic feelings roiling inside her spilled out.

His gaze was enigmatic. "Tonight, we will have dinner in the village."

"You didn't bring me all the way to Greece for dinner, Christos."

He reached out, almost as if he couldn't help it, and dragged a finger over her cheek. She did not recoil, though a part of her knew she should. It was a triumph simply to stand there and not lean into his touch when she so desperately wanted to do so.

"Patience, Lucillitsa. You must learn patience."

More than that, she realized, she needed to learn how to stop this flame that writhed in her soul at the simplest of his touches.

Lucilla went to her room—a very spacious and well-appointed room—and worked on her computer, which Christos had also returned. The emails about the aborted shareholders' meeting were fast and furious, but mostly everyone accepted the delay and got on with their business. She had a few emails from Antonio, asking if she'd uncovered anything useful, and a couple of reports on events happening in the coming week. Perhaps the most surprising thing was the announcement that Sophie, Christos's assistant, needed to take extended leave for personal reasons. Jessie had assured her in an email, cc'ing Christos, that she was happy to cover in Sophie's absence, until the situation could be firmly resolved.

Lucilla had set everything up so that it should run smoothly without her, even when her absence was unexpected. It chafed to be here when she hadn't expected to be—and yet the beauty of the land outside the windows also called to her. She hadn't taken a vacation in so long, and the lemon-scented air was driving her crazy. She found a bikini in among the things Christos had bought for her and thought about putting it on and heading out to the pool.

Before she could do so, she heard a splash and she went out on the balcony and looked at the pool below. Christos cut through the water so gracefully that she found herself mesmerized. He reached one end, did a flip turn and then propelled himself back to the other side. He kept swimming, back and forth, back and forth, until she wondered how much longer he could last. Eventually, he swam over to the infinity edge and propped his elbows on it, gazing out at the landscape and sea beyond. He didn't seem to realize she was watching, and she let herself look at him as long as she wanted.

His back was to her. He was dark-skinned, his muscles well defined and glistening with water. His jet hair was slicked to his head, and she found herself studying the lines of his skull. When he turned to the side, his profile was even more striking than usual. He swam to the end and lifted himself out. He was breathing hard, water running down his body, and she felt that little flutter in her belly that always happened when he was near.

Lucilla ducked back inside, her heart hammering. Then she heard him almost beneath her window, speaking to someone in Greek. She crept back out to look down. He'd toweled off and now stood there with his back to her, his phone to his ear.

They'd slept together but it had been so dark that she hadn't really seen him. Looking at his body now was almost too much. He was beautiful, but she hadn't expected anything less. Her eyes drifted down over his back, his firm butt, his legs. He stepped out into the sunshine again and she nearly gasped.

The skin of his back was crisscrossed by fine, silvery scars. They weren't noticeable at first, kind of like an impressionist painting where the strokes weren't distinguishable from the complete picture until you looked hard enough. Or until the light hit them just right.

Her heart squeezed into a tight knot in her chest. Why hadn't she felt them that night? How could she have been so intimate with him and not known the marks he bore? Was she truly that oblivious?

He spun around and Lucilla ducked back inside again. Her chest was tight and her stomach hurt as she tried to process what she'd seen. How did anyone get those kinds of marks and not suffer an incredible amount of pain?

And she had slapped him earlier. It did not feel so good now as it had then. In fact, it made her stomach churn that she'd assaulted him, no matter the inducement.

She went back to her computer and tried to work. But she couldn't stop thinking about Christos and how he'd gotten those scars. When it was finally time for dinner, she dressed in a vibrant tangerine chiffon dress she found in the closet and paired it with jeweled low-heeled sandals. She was shorter than she liked when she walked into the foyer to meet Christos, who stood there so tall and proud and remote.

She already felt small next to him, but the low heels made her feel more so. Christos was dressed in a pair of khaki trousers and a black shirt and her mouth watered at the slice of his tanned skin visible in the open neck. Her eyes searched his, but he said nothing that indicated he knew she'd seen his back today. He'd had many lovers, naturally, which meant he probably didn't go around hiding his scars.

But she wanted to know where they'd come from. How did a person get so many? Did he have others? What else had she missed?

"You look beautiful, Lucillitsa."

Her ears grew hot. She didn't want to crave his compliments. "Thank you. And what is with this new name, Christos? What does this one mean?"

It was the second time he'd called her that, and she wondered. Not only that, but she secretly loved the way he said the word, his accent rolling over the sounds in such a way that she felt as if he were stroking her skin.

"It means 'little Lucilla.'"

For some reason, that made her palms sweat. "All right, baby," she said softly, though her pulse hummed dangerously fast.

He only grinned at her. Then he ushered her out the door and into a sleek Mercedes coupe. He put the top up with the press of a button and then they zoomed out the driveway and onto a narrow stretch of road that zipped between rocky cliffs before giving way to a long stretch where she could see the ocean spread out on one side and the island on the other.

It took them about fifteen minutes to arrive at the village. Christos parked and then came around to help her out. The sun was still in the sky, but it was setting quickly. The village, it turned out, was not so small as she'd thought. She'd only been able to see a small part of it from the villa on the hill, but the village was more of a small city, fanning outward from the harbor. The buildings were a mixture of white ones and colored ones like salmon and pale ocher. Christos strolled down the streets slowly so that she could take in the sights.

They walked past a street where children played and Christos stopped, his shoulders stiff as he stared down the alley. The buildings were a little shabbier here. Washing hung high above the street, stretched between the buildings, and women sat in the doorways, peeling vegetables and chatting back and forth. The children were small and dirty, but that was no shock since they were children. She'd often had to threaten her smaller siblings when they were younger if she'd wanted them to wash up for dinner.

Lucilla moved closer to Christos. She wasn't certain why, but she had an urge to slip her hand into his and tug him away. She did not, however.

"I had forgotten," he said.

"Forgotten what?"

He shook himself as he looked down at her. His expression was taut. "It's nothing. Come, I've promised you dinner."

He took her arm and tucked it in his and started down the street again. She didn't try to pull away. She could feel the tension in him, but she didn't know what to say. They arrived at a taverna set alongside the picturesque square and Christos procured them a table near the edge. A band sat in the square, playing bouzoukis, tambourines and mandolins among other instruments. It was beautiful music, different than what she was used to, and she felt a lightness that she should not feel considering the circumstances of her presence in Greece.

The waiter came by and Christos ordered in Greek without asking her what she wanted. It annoyed her—but then she got over it, because the night was too pretty and the music too lovely and she actually felt relaxed, which was insane. But it was a feeling she wanted to hold on to as long as possible.

The wine arrived and Lucilla sipped hers. It was crisp and lovely and went down easily.

"You are enjoying the music?"

"Yes." And she was, truly. A small breeze wafted over her, coming in from the harbor that lay not too far away. She took another sip of wine and frowned. She had to remember that this was not a vacation. That she'd been brought here to see something he considered important enough to trade his severance package for. The atmosphere lured her to forget, but she couldn't let that happen.

"I'm afraid I don't understand why I'm here, Christos. I'm waiting for you to tell me."

And wondering if it had anything to do with those scars. She shivered inside, wanting to reach for his hand and just squeeze it in hers.

"I grew up here," he said after a long while, his eyes far away. "And not in the house where we are staying, as you may well have imagined." He turned the full force of his gaze on her then and she tried not to reach for him. She did not quite succeed. Her fingers brushed his. And then she pulled her hand away and tucked it in her lap while the other clutched her wineglass.

He sucked in a breath. "That street… We lived on

that street. My father was a fisherman and my mother was a housewife. I was their only child."

She had read the report about domestic disturbances at his house, but she'd never really considered what that might mean. Yes, she'd pictured violent arguments and maybe a few slaps. That was not okay, but what he'd done…

"I know your father was violent," she said, trying to give him a way into it.

His laugh was bitter. "Everyone knew that, *glykia mou.* And yet it still did not save my mother. Or me."

Tears pressed against her eyelids. She sucked them back, but then the food arrived and she was able to concentrate on that instead. Christos said no more about his family. Indeed, he seemed to relax a bit.

But though she didn't cry, she was on edge in a way she hadn't expected. She wanted to know what he had to tell her, and she felt simultaneously like she was intruding on his privacy. She knew things she wished she didn't. And there were still those scars.

They were silent so long that his voice came as a surprise. "You lost your mother when you were young, yes?"

She looked up from the moussaka, her stomach suddenly cold. "Yes."

"What happened?"

She wanted to tell him it was none of his business, to say she didn't talk about it—but how could she say such things when she already knew so much about him, and not because he'd told her himself? It was business, she told herself. *Business.* And yet she felt more and more as if she'd violated his privacy with her investigation.

Lucilla swallowed the sudden lump in her throat. "She

walked out one day and never came back. We haven't heard from her in about twenty years now."

"I'm sorry."

She took a sip of the wine to cover her discomfort. "She suffered from postnatal depression. And after she had Cara, I don't think she ever recovered. It just got to be too much for her. So she left."

"How old were you?"

"Fourteen." She toyed with her fork, pushing food around without eating it. "I raised Cara, you know. I was her surrogate mother, except I didn't really know how to be a mother, so I did a lot wrong. If she's impulsive, it's my fault."

"It's not your fault, Lucilla. Your parents shoulder much of the blame. Your mother for abandoning her children, your father for letting you, a child yourself, raise a baby."

She dropped the fork, her mouth suddenly dry. "Why are we talking about me? I thought this was about you."

"It's about both of us. You lost your mother at fourteen, and it was difficult for you. I lost mine, too. But for a far different reason."

He didn't say anything else and she wanted to scream. "I told you what happened to mine. Are you going to return the favor?"

His eyes glittered in the lights that were turning on with the setting of the sun. "Are you finished eating?"

She looked down at her plate and knew she couldn't eat another bite. "Yes."

"Then I will return the favor. But not here."

Christos flagged the waiter over. He paid the bill and then he helped her up and took her by the hand. She didn't protest as he led her alongside the harbor to

where the fishing boats were kept. They rocked gently
in their moorings while men called to one another as
they mended nets, adjusted ropes and readied fishing
gear for in the morning.

Christos continued down the path beside the harbor
until they reached a building. She didn't realize it was
a church until they went inside. He stopped and made
the sign of the cross, which surprised her, and then led
her forward into the interior. The church was small,
but the windows were stained glass. The dome soared
above their heads, painted with frescoes that had faded
over the years.

They didn't stop, however. Christos led her into the
cemetery and then over to what she realized was an ossuary. The skulls and bones of hundreds of people were
stacked in neat rows one on top of the other beneath a
half dome. The ossuary was behind bars to prevent anyone from getting inside. It was strangely beautiful to
stand there and see the yellowed bones of people who
had once been as alive as she.

"My mother is here," Christos said, his voice soft and
sad as he pointed at the ossuary.

Shock rooted her to the spot. Not that his mother
was dead, which saddened her, but that she was a part
of what Lucilla had assumed was an anonymous collection of bones.

Christos looked down at her. "In Greece, we do not
cremate. We bury the dead in graves, but only for a
while. There isn't enough land, you see. Once someone's time is up, they are put here unless the family is
very rich and can afford a permanent grave. And I was
not back then."

"I'm sorry." She didn't know what else to say. She

told herself that it was terrible his mother was dead, but what did that have to do with running her company and getting him to leave?

And yet she couldn't help but feel terrible for him. She had no idea where her own mother was—Was she alive? Dead? Where?—and she probably never would. Christos knew where his mother was—and yet he didn't. That thought floored her. He could point to the ossuary and know she was there—but not where, not who.

His voice was anguished. "I think I killed her. Me and my father both. He did the physical work of breaking her, and I did the rest when I broke him."

She reached for his hand and squeezed it hard. He was so warm and vibrant and alive—and yet he seemed far away from her right now. Lost in a hell of his own making. "I'm so sorry. I don't know the right words to say to you, but I am sorry."

He lifted her hand to his mouth and kissed the back of it. Heat flared deep inside. "I believe you are, Lucilla." He tugged in a deep, ragged breath. And then the words tumbled out of him while she stood there and ached as if they were poison darts.

"My father raped her. I was not what she wanted, and yet she loved me, anyway. She married him to provide a life for me. And I couldn't stop him from hurting her, from beating her and breaking her spirit. Until one day I could. I was fourteen, and he'd just beaten her bloody. Her jaw was broken, her arm. I walked in too late. But I grabbed the first thing I could find—the club he'd just beaten her with—and I used it on him."

"Christos—" She couldn't stop the tears from spilling over this time. They slid down her cheeks, hot and wet and bitterly painful. She could feel the tremors moving over him, and she just wanted to hold him. But she wasn't sure he would allow it.

"He never beat her again. You are right that I nearly killed him. I wanted to, believe me. But I stopped because she begged me to." He dragged in a breath. "There is more I could show you. More I could tell you. But I find I no longer have the stomach for it."

CHAPTER ELEVEN

HE NEVER TALKED about these things with anyone, and yet he was telling her. He'd told himself, when he'd concocted his plan to bring her to Greece, that he was doing so to protect everything he'd built. He'd intended to start in Kefalonia and then move on to Athens, to show her the dirt and squalor of his teen years. But he no longer cared about protecting anything. He only cared that she was crying and he'd made her do so.

She'd lost her mother at the same age he had gone to prison and effectively lost his own. By the time he'd been released at eighteen, his mother had returned to Kefalonia and died of a broken heart.

"Lucillitsa," he murmured, bringing her into the curve of his embrace. She curled her fists into his shirt and cried softly. He stared over her head, at the ossuary, and his own eyes blurred.

Vlakas. What had he been thinking to bring her here? He was a fool for doing so. It did nothing except upset her and scrape off the thin layer of veneer protecting his emotions. Anywhere else, he was impervious. But when he returned to Kefalonia, when he walked into this church—which he had not done in several years now—the pain was as raw and ragged as the first time he'd come.

They stood that way for a long time. Finally, she spoke. "I'm sorry. I don't know why I'm so upset."

He rubbed her back. "Because you are tenderhearted, no matter that you are tough on the outside."

She tilted her head back to look up at him. Her eyes were filled with pain and sorrow and he wanted to kiss those feelings away. He was angry with her for threatening him, his career and future, and yet as he stood here and held her, he could hardly remember that it was so.

"I didn't mean to hurt you, Christos. I just wanted you to step aside and give me back my company."

He stroked his thumbs over her cheeks, removing the wetness. Her lashes were spiky with tears and her eyes were so wide and earnest. He wanted her, though he should not.

"I am not the one who took it away from you, *glykia mou*."

Her fingers tightened in his shirt and he knew he'd touched a sore spot. "I know. But I wanted it nonetheless. I need to prove to him…"

Her chin dropped and he found himself staring at the top of her head. In her own way, she was as lost as he was. She smelled so lovely, like flowers and sunshine. He stepped back and took her hand as something twisted deep inside him.

"Come, let's leave this place."

She glanced over at the ossuary, at the rows of skulls staring empty-eyed back at them, and pulled in a shaky breath.

"Of course."

They walked back through the cemetery, through the

church and out onto the street. Christos dragged air into his lungs, unaware how tight they'd felt in the cemetery until just now.

Lucilla's hand tightened on his. "Are you all right?"

"Mostly," he told her, his voice clipped.

He didn't expect her to slip her arms around his waist and hug him tight, but that's precisely what she did. He let himself hold her again, let his head fall until he could bury his face in her hair and breathe in her sweet scent. His body began to stir. He sensed when her breathing changed, sensed when the heat that always simmered between them began to flare and grow inside her.

Her breathing came in short little bursts now and her fingers moved over the shirt on his back, smoothing it as if she needed something rhythmical to do.

He needed to kiss her. He needed it more than he needed his next breath. He tipped her head back with a finger and pressed his mouth to hers. She gasped, but then she opened and met his tongue with her own.

He could drown in this woman, he thought. He could sink so deeply into her that he never resurfaced. And right now he didn't care. They kissed deeply, passionately, their tongues tangling, their bodies straining to touch as they wrapped themselves around each other. He shifted his hips against her, brought his aching erection against the V of her thighs, and exulted in her gasp.

But then he forced himself to step away, before he lifted her skirts and took her against the side of the church on a darkened street where anyone could happen along. She made a little noise—of frustration, of regret or self-recrimination, he did not know. All he knew was that he wanted her.

"I'm taking you back to the villa," he told her, his

voice ragged with need. "And, Lucilla, I'm taking you to bed. If that's not what you want, then you need to say so now."

She sounded breathless. "And what would you do if I said no? Leave me here?"

His stomach clenched. "Of course not. But I would drop you at the door and keep driving."

Her eyes flashed. "And do what? Find a companion for the evening?"

He barely suppressed a groan. "Lucillitsa, I am a grown man, capable of dealing with an erection without needing to blindly use it on the nearest female. If you say no, I'll live. But I won't be happy about it."

She stepped into his space again, tilted her head up to look at him as she ran her fingers over his jaw. "God knows I *should* say no. But I can't. I want to be with you, Christos. As soon as possible."

He grabbed her hand and hurried back toward the town square and his car. It was a few minutes walking, but they reached it in almost record time. He started the powerful engine and raced through the streets, heading for the long climb back to his house that perched like a silent watchman over the sea.

Just a few minutes and she would be his again. He would possess her on his big, lonely bed with the sounds of the sea crashing into the rocks below. He would take her so thoroughly she would never forget this night.

Christos roared around a corner—and screeched to a halt. A herd of goats ranged across the road, bleating and staring into the headlights with spookily iridescent eyes. They were in no hurry to move, so he reversed and shot back down the road and up another that led to a secluded overlook. He shoved the car into park and got out. Then he wrenched open Lucilla's door and pulled her into his arms before backing her against the side of the car.

His mouth dropped to her shoulder and she gasped. "What are we doing here, Christos?"

"I don't want to wait," he said, his fingers going to the zipper at her back. He tugged it down until the bodice of her dress fell free. Overhead the stars filled the sky like millions of fireflies winking against a velvet blanket. A slice of moon hung low in the sky, painting the sea with a pearly brush.

Lucilla's breasts were pushed up high in the bra, their creamy swells inviting him to lick them where they touched. He dipped his tongue into the hollow between them and then across one soft mound. She gasped and clutched his shoulders and he felt exultant inside. He reached behind her and unsnapped the bra, dropping it inside the car. Her breasts fell free, their crests budding tight, beckoning his mouth.

He cupped them in his palms, dipped his head to suck one perfect nipple between his lips.

"Christos… Oh, I can't think when you do that…."

"Don't think," he murmured. "Don't do anything but feel."

He finished unzipping her dress and then let it fall. She gasped when it did, and he caught it, urged her to step out of it so he could toss it inside the car. Not that he wanted to take time for that, but she wasn't going to appreciate him trampling her clothing in the dirt.

"You, too," she said. "I want to touch you."

Her fingers were on his buttons and he let her work them while he continued to make love to her breasts. She was so sensitive, so lovely. And then she shoved his shirt off his shoulders, and he let it fall, uncaring about his own clothing.

Her hands slid over his skin, touching and probing, and pleasure buzzed inside him. His body needed hers so badly, but he couldn't take her roughly when he was already planning to take her against the side of a car. She deserved better, but he was unable to wait for the time it would have taken them to go the long way around to his house.

He dropped to his knees in front of her, framing her hips with his hands. Her panties were a tiny scrap of silk that he pulled down until she could step free. These he dropped, uncaring where they landed.

"Christos, you aren't—"

"I am," he said firmly, pressing a kiss to the curls at the apex of her thighs. He felt the shiver rack her body then and he knew she needed him as much as he needed her. He glided his hands up her inner thighs, parted her with his fingers and licked the bud of her sex as she cried out.

She fisted a hand in his hair. The other clutched the side of the Mercedes, presumably because her knees were weak. God, he hoped her knees were weak. He lifted one of her legs and propped it on his shoulder. And then he ran his tongue the length of her, tasting her thoroughly.

She began to moan as he relentlessly tasted her, darting his tongue inside her, then around her clitoris until she started rocking her hips to get him where she wanted him. He tightened his focus to the tiny, sensitive button of flesh while she moved against him, her hand on the back of his head now, directing him. He clutched her bottom in his hands, held her firmly while he drove her toward the edge of her own personal cliff. He wanted her to come, wanted her to explode and scream his name into the night.

He felt her stiffen—and then she did precisely that, her body jerking as his name broke from her lips. It filled him with satisfaction—and an overwhelming urge to be inside her while she shattered around him the next time.

He shot to his feet and unzipped his trousers, freeing himself. Then he lifted her against him. She wrapped her legs around him as he pressed her back against the car. Her body was still shuddering when he found her entrance and thrust inside her.

Her inner muscles clamped down on him as he swallowed hard and tried not to lose himself with the first thrust. He found his control—barely—and then pulled out of her before slamming back in again.

Lucilla moaned as he repeated the motion. His blood pounded in his ears as the tension gathered low in his spine. She rolled herself forward, sought his mouth as she wrapped her arms around him. He kissed her, their teeth clashing almost painfully with the force of their joining. He gentled the kiss, but he did not gentle his possession of her body. She was so hot and wet and warm, and his skin was on fire with the need to make her call his name again.

But somewhere along the way he lost his control, his body giving in to the sensations rioting through him. He felt as if his skin was about to curl into a crisp as he slammed into her, deeper and harder than before. He held her hips hard, pressed her against the Mercedes and used her body for his pleasure.

And for hers, he realized when her muscles tightened and she cried his name once more. It was almost a sob, a plea, and his heart filled with the need to cherish her, to worship her. He thrust into her several more times—and then jerked out of her at the last minute, spilling himself on her thigh.

Lucilla had never had sex like that in her life. It had been so raw, so edgy—so necessary to breathing and living—that thinking about it on the long car ride back to his villa had her wound into knots by the time they arrived.

They hadn't spoken in the aftermath. He'd handed her the dress, helped her pull it up and zip it. She'd forgone the bra, and it seemed as if her panties were lost for all time somewhere on Kefalonian soil.

Christos had yanked his trousers up and zipped them, then found his shirt and tossed it into the back of the car. He'd kissed her once, swiftly, then swatted her lightly on the bottom and helped her into the seat before going around to his side.

They coasted into the garage of his home and then went into the darkened house. Her brain whirled. What had she been thinking to have sex with him again? Was she crazy? And, even more insane, when could she do it again?

She wanted to drop her head into her hands and groan. Everything she desired for her career and her family was within reach if she would only walk away. But she couldn't. God help her, but from the moment she'd stood beside that ossuary with him, she'd lost her strength of will to walk away.

He stopped in the moonlit living room and turned to her. She stood there with her bra and purse in her hands, her stomach clenching, and waited.

"I apologize for being rough," he said, and she put her

fingers over his mouth to stop him. She'd loved every moment of what he'd done to her. He'd taught her things about herself, about her body and her pleasure, that had been more of a revelation than she would have thought possible at this point in her life.

"Please don't ruin this night by apologizing. I think what just happened between us is probably the most honest we've been with each other. I liked it. A lot."

He swept her against him and took her mouth, gently this time. Just that light, sweet kiss sent the butterflies swirling again as she relived the beautiful strength of his lovemaking just minutes ago. As long as she lived, she would never forget the Greek night spread above them like a sheltering cape or the sound of his voice when he uttered her name in his moment of crisis.

"I want more, Lucillitsa. As much as you can give me for the rest of the night."

She tried not to focus on that one phrase—*the rest of the night*—while her heart managed to beat faster and ache all at the same time. He was confusing, this man, and somehow so very necessary at the same time.

"I want more, too."

She thought he might lead her to his room and gently undress her, but he swept her into his arms and carried her through the house, up the stairs and into the large master bedroom. He set her down and undressed her quickly, then undressed himself, and they fell onto the bed in a tangle of arms and legs and hot, wet kisses. This time he sheathed himself, and then he was inside her, stroking into her as perfectly as he had before.

Only this time—this time—she felt the sweetness of their joining all the way to her heart.

CHAPTER TWELVE

THIS TIME WHEN Lucilla woke, she was not alone. Christos lay beside her, his big body stretched out, an arm above his head as he lay on his stomach. Sometime in the night, one of them had thrown the covers off. She propped herself on an elbow and studied the strong lines of his shoulders and the total perfection of his features where his face turned toward her.

There was a pinch in her heart that was not characteristic as she looked at him. Somewhere in the night, her world had shifted on its axis—and everything became sharper and clearer than before, as if she'd been viewing the world through the wrong magnification and someone had turned the dials.

She didn't want to analyze the warm, possessive feelings flooding through her as she looked at him, or the wave of sympathy as she thought of him in the cemetery. She sat up and looked closely at his back, at the web of his scars where they crossed and recrossed, weaving a tapestry of pain.

"What are you doing, *agapi mou?*"

She started, her skin tingling with heat that he'd caught her. There was nothing for it but to confess. "I'm looking at your back, Christos."

He rolled over and put both hands behind his head. He was gloriously, beautifully naked—and this was the first time she'd seen him that way in full daylight. His thick shaft lay against his leg—and it was beginning to stir. Her belly churned with fresh butterflies.

"I have something you can look at," he said, and her eyes whipped to his to find him grinning lazily.

"I like looking at all of you."

He grabbed her and pulled her on top of him, until they were pressed full length against each other. Oh, the heat of his skin on hers was marvelous. Decadent. Had she ever been this casual with another lover?

"And I like *feeling* all of you," he told her, his voice making her tingle in all the right places.

She lifted her hand and pushed hair back from his forehead. His eyes were hooded as he watched her and she couldn't make out what he felt—other than lust, which was patently obvious the way his penis kept growing against her abdomen.

"I want to know what happened to you," she whispered, and his eyes shuttered. Just like that, all the warmth left them and she knew she'd gone too far. But he'd brought her here to tell her things and she wanted to know. Needed to know in order to understand him.

"You can't guess?"

She traced her finger over his lips. "Your father?"

Now his eyes were glittering with heat. Angry heat. "Of course. He was a cruel man. He liked to cause pain."

Her father had generally ignored her and her siblings after her mother left, and she'd always thought that was cruel in a way. How naive she'd been. Her father hadn't been cruel so much as self-absorbed and casually indifferent to his children's needs. He wasn't a monster; he was just a flawed man.

"I'm sorry I hit you," she said, her throat tight.

"I've had worse." Christos flipped her onto her back, his body hard and insistent against hers. "Have I told you enough now, *agapi mou?* Is there anything else I can do for you, any other way I can strip my soul bare for your curiosity?"

His voice had an edge to it that should have worried her. In the few short months he'd been at the Chatsfield, the one thing she knew about him was that he did not get emotional. And yet this man had shown her sides of himself she hadn't known existed last night.

"I'm not trying to hurt you. I just… I care." Especially when she'd been the one to force him to confront this part of his life again.

He dropped his gaze to her bare breasts. "I'd rather not talk about this right now," he murmured thickly.

Could she blame him? Her heart ached for him and her soul wanted to comfort his. She only knew one way to do that. What he needed right now was the physical connection between them. He would not accept her pity, but he would accept the comfort of her body.

"Then we won't talk. Make love to me, Christos. That's what you can do for me right now."

He entered her body in a single thrust and her eyes snapped closed at the intensity of it. He filled her, made her crave nothing but this. Right now, this moment, she would give anything she had to feel like this for the rest of her life. It was so unexpected that tears sprang against the backs of her eyes. She'd set out to ruin him but perhaps she'd ruined herself instead.

His cheek against hers was everything she needed in this world. She turned her head and kissed him as the tears she'd been holding in escaped and trickled down her cheeks.

His voice was suddenly strangled as he lifted himself above her. "Lucilla *mou,* don't. You tear me apart when you cry."

"I don't mean to." It was almost a sob.

He bracketed her cheeks between his broad hands and kissed away her tears—and her heart broke open with everything she felt and everything she'd been trying to contain. Somehow, she'd fallen in love with him. With this man who infuriated her and challenged her and made her feel incredibly sexy and alive. Everyone thought Christos was cold and unemotional, but she knew the truth. He'd cut himself off because he'd been hurt and he kept himself apart because he didn't know how to trust anyone.

She wanted him to trust her. To love her. Lucilla shivered with the strength of her emotions—and the fear that she could lose everything if he wasn't capable of returning those feelings.

She threaded her fingers into his hair and brought his mouth to hers. She kissed him brutally, desperately. She couldn't bear to have him be tender right now, not when her heart was so fragile. She needed his strength and his passion, his overwhelming virility.

He held her hard against him, his kiss matching her own. She could feel his heart pounding in his chest but she dared not hope it was for the same reason hers pounded.

"Lucillitsa," he groaned when she shifted her hips.

"I want to fly, Christos," she whispered. "Make me fly."

* * *

They spent the next couple of days wrapped up in each other, but Christos knew they would have to return soon. The emails and phone calls from the office were increasing, though neither of them liked to talk about it. Right now they were supposed to be on a tour of Chatsfield locations, not lounging in bed together in the middle of the afternoon.

So many things remained unsaid between them. It could not keep going this way, but he was reluctant to bring reality back into their relationship. He did not do long term, but he could see making an exception for Lucilla. Just for a while, of course. Not forever. He definitely did not do forever. The mere idea made him go ice-cold with dread.

And yet the idea of letting her go also made him cold. He did not like feeling these contradictory emotions. Not at all.

It was the chaotic state of his thoughts that led him to start the conversation at dinner that night. They'd returned to the taverna to eat and, this time, perhaps enjoy the experience a bit more. But he found he wasn't enjoying it the way he should.

He couldn't quite keep his eyes from straying to Lucilla as she sat and watched the band in the square. Her face was so expressive, especially when she thought no one was watching her. She was beautiful and almost carefree, which annoyed him since he felt as if he were weighted down by cares at the moment.

The strains of the Zeibekiko began and Lucilla's eyes widened a moment later.

"What is happening?" she asked, glancing over at him.

Christos turned to look. A man had started to dance—

alone, as was traditional—and it was clear his dance was for a woman who sat near. She smiled and clapped and the man whirled and glided in his own rhythm. He snapped his fingers, stepped back and forth, and shot smoldering looks at his lady.

The woman looked happy, and the man—well, the man looked intense and determined. And more than a little bit in love with the woman.

"It is a Zeibekiko. He dances for her."

Lucilla's breath shortened. "Oh, how romantic."

Yes, it was—or could be. Christos did not look again. Instead, he took some bills from his wallet and laid them on the table.

"Let's go," he said, and her gaze snapped to his. Her brow knit with confusion—and then with worry. He felt like an ass, but he stood and took her hand and they walked away from the dancing man and his lady.

"That was lovely," she said. "Is it traditional for a man to dance for his sweetheart?"

"It can be, yes." He wasn't sure why he didn't want to discuss this with her, but he didn't. That couple looked happy, in love, and Christos had no idea what that was like. Or why anyone would want it. And he didn't want to think about it.

They walked back to the car in silence. Lucilla turned to him as he reached for her door, stopping him with a palm on his chest. "What's the matter, Christos?"

He hated that she could read him so well. "Nothing is the matter."

"I don't believe you." Her voice was soft and sweet and he despised himself for craving her. This was not his way. This was not how he did things. He'd brought her here to save himself—and even to punish her for digging into his life—but he'd not intended to need her so much. Since that moment in the cemetery, he'd been thinking that she made him feel less alone in the world.

But it was dangerous to feel that way because he knew how easily things could change. He'd had a mother and then he hadn't. He'd been a kid and then he'd been a prisoner. He only knew extremes.

And it was time to get back to his life the way he understood it. He had to put an end to this, swiftly and ruthlessly. The same as he did everything. There was no sense in prolonging their stay.

"We've been here for a few days, Lucilla. It's time to move on. I have a company to run and you have a job to do, as well."

It was out there now, the assumption that he was still the CEO of the Chatsfield empire. He'd thrown it at her like a challenge and he waited to see what she would do. If she threatened him, then he would know, wouldn't he? He could forget this inconvenient attraction and move on with a clear mind. He almost wished she would.

"Yes, I realize. We are meant to be on a tour of the other locations."

"We are. But I think we should go back to London. I'll need you to run things there while I continue the tour as planned."

He didn't miss the hurt in her eyes. He hadn't planned to say that, but it suddenly occurred to him that he needed time away from her if he was to renew his focus on what his life was supposed to be.

Her gaze dropped away from his and she swallowed. He had a sudden urge to fall to his knees and beg her to forgive him. Which meant that he wouldn't do it, of course. He stiffened his spine and waited for her reaction.

"All right."

Suddenly, the emotions churning inside him reached a boiling point. She'd violated his privacy—violated his solitude, damn her—and now she was going to just take whatever he dished out as if she hadn't gone to extraordinary lengths to topple him? It was her fault he was feeling like he'd been turned inside out. Her fault he couldn't find his footing in this emotional quicksand.

"That's it, Lucilla? You're prepared to accept my leadership now? No more threats or tantrums?"

She looked stunned. And then she looked angry. "Tantrums? Are you kidding me? Because I've disagreed with you in the past, I'm throwing tantrums?"

He almost rejoiced at seeing fiery Lucilla make her reappearance. And yet he had to be strong and firm with her if he were to get the Chatsfield—and his life—back on track. "I don't care what you call them, but I prefer we not disagree in front of the staff."

Her eyes flashed. "I will disagree with you whenever I feel like it. And no, I'm not going to threaten you."

She sucked in a breath then and he thought she might be dangerously close to crying. He wanted to drag her into his arms and apologize—but he was frozen by conflicting feelings. Why was it so hard to do what he knew needed to be done? It was kinder to them both if he let her go now. If he didn't string her along with false hopes for the future.

Her chin lifted in that way he'd come to realize meant she was determined. "You're the Chatsfield CEO, Christos. Because my father chose you, and while I don't agree, I have to accept his decision. But I will *not* blindly follow your orders just because you've made me feel ashamed of myself for trying to use your past against you. I won't do that. Ever. But I damn well will tell you when you're being a stupid ass."

She grabbed the handle and yanked the car door open. Then she got inside and shot him a look as she reached for the door. "Oh, yeah," she said. "You are currently being a stupid ass."

And then she slammed the door.

When they reached the house perched on its lonely cliff, Lucilla went to the room she'd woken up in on the first day. She hadn't slept in that bed since, having spent the past few nights with Christos, but she was far too angry to go to bed with him now. He didn't stop her, and that only added to her misery as she stomped up the stairs.

Her heart hurt and her eyes stung with unshed tears. She'd been having so much fun tonight, enjoying the food and music and being with him. Just being with him. She loved it when he smiled—which hadn't been often tonight—when he ordered for her in Greek and even when he opened her car door and set her inside with a kiss on her hand as they were leaving the house earlier.

She went over to the double doors that opened onto the balcony, wrenching them open and going out into the warm Greek night. Oh, God, what had she been thinking? Why had she told him she wanted him that night when he'd taken her to the cemetery? If she'd just kept her emotions in check, she could have walked out of this time in Greece with her heart intact.

No, you couldn't.

She shoved the evil voice deep and sucked in a breath, and then another and another as she tried not to cry.

Damn him, and damn her for being so needy. He'd made her feel things she never had with another man, and she'd let her heart run wild and free.

Now look at her. Christos only cared about the job, about making sure she wouldn't use the information she'd found against him, while she cared about *him*. About his happiness.

She clenched her fists on the railing. Oh, it hurt to love. She'd never been in love with anyone before. She'd loved her family, but she'd sacrificed so damn much for them. She'd sacrificed all her youthful dreams, her hopes, even her thoughts of love and happiness and children with a man. She'd never allowed herself to fall before—or maybe she hadn't been capable of it.

But she was now, and she had, and for the worst man possible. Christos did not love her. If he did, he wouldn't have been so cold and unemotional just now. He only cared about the job—and she thought too much of herself to beg him for even a crumb of affection.

She would not do that. Not ever. He clearly wanted it to be over. He wanted her to return to London and run the company while he toured the locations alone. She hadn't expected that. She put her hands to her hot cheeks and vowed not to cry.

Dammit, what *had* she expected? That everything would go back to normal, with the exception of their relationship? That they'd need one room while they toured rather than two?

What an idiot she was. Christos was the ultimate manipulator, bringing her here and forcing her to confront the circumstances of his youth. He'd known how she would react, she had no doubt. Because that's what he did. He observed and cataloged and calculated. And

he'd made himself into a spectacular businessman because of it.

No, she would not expose him now. She couldn't.
What was there to expose? That he'd been another person? That his father beat him so badly he still bore the
scars? That he'd gone to juvenile detention for nearly
killing a man who would have killed him and his mother
eventually?

Only a cruel person would do that. And she was not
cruel. Perhaps that was her downfall. Perhaps she wasn't
willing to do whatever it took to succeed. She sniffed.
At least she could live with herself.

But she could not stay here. Not for another moment. She went back inside and changed into a pair of
jeans and a comfortable silky shirt. Then she grabbed a
sweater, picked up her purse and briefcase and headed
downstairs.

The doors were open to the terrace and she went outside, found Christos standing beside the pool with a glass
in one hand. He looked lost and alone, but she hardened
her heart and swore she would not try to soothe him. He
did not want her comfort. He did not want her.

He turned as he heard her feet falling on the stone.
She did not give him a chance to speak.

"I want to leave now." Her heart hammered and her
pulse beat wildly in her ears. She thought she probably sounded a touch desperate, a touch insane, but she
couldn't spend another night in this house, not with him
in another room and her knowing that she would never
spend a night in his arms again. That it was over and
she was the fool for falling.

"Now? It's after eleven at night."

"So? You said I could go when I was ready. I'm ready.

Call a helicopter, Christos. Call a damn speedboat. I don't care, but I want to leave."

"Lucillitsa—"

"Don't you dare," she bit out. Her chest heaved with emotion. "Don't you dare call me anything other than Lucilla or Ms. Chatsfield *ever* again. You've made it very clear that we are done, so no more cutesy names. No more intimacy. It's over, Christos, and I want to leave."

"You are overreacting." He sounded cool, emotionless. Mechanical.

"Am I?" She felt wild inside, crazy with emotion. She wanted to slap him again, and that was an awful thing to feel. And she wanted to wrap her arms around his waist and beg him to love her. That was perhaps a *worse* thing to feel. She'd been at low points in her life, at points where she felt no one cared or understood, but none of those moments compared to this one.

To standing here in front of the man she loved and knowing he didn't feel the same for her. To trying to hold herself together while simultaneously knowing she *had* to get off this island before she exploded.

"Morning is soon enough," he began.

"No. Now, Christos. You brought me here against my will and now I want to go. *Right now.*"

He stared at her for a long minute. For one wild moment, she hoped he would relent, that his stony facade would crumble and he would drag her into his arms and kiss her. That he would tell her he was a fool and beg her forgiveness.

Those things did not happen.

"Very well," he said, fishing into his pocket for his phone. "I'll make it happen."

CHAPTER THIRTEEN

LUCILLA COULD HARDLY believe she was back in London. She'd been home for a week, and she'd been battling a sense of unreality ever since. It was as if her life could be divided into two halves: before Greece and after Greece. As if it were that simple. As if it came down to a single moment where everything had changed when in fact it was a vortex of change that spun her apart and then put her back together again.

Though not the same as before.

The world was sharper now, crueler, and she was battered and bruised. But she was still here, dammit, and she would survive. No one knew how her life had been ripped apart at the seams and she had no intentions of letting them know.

Just like always, she was Lucilla Chatsfield, the rock upon which her entire family could rely. She had met up with Cara recently at the Demarche event, but seeing Cara hadn't grounded her in the way it used to. That her siblings no longer seemed to need her as much as they once had was not a problem for her. She would be available, like always. For a brief time, Christos had made her think of herself—her wants and needs and desires—but she was over that now.

It hurt too much to put herself first, so she would bury herself in work again and hope the sharpness of her agony would settle into a dull roar.

Lucilla sniffed as she scrolled through the morning reports. Since Christos was off gallivanting around the world, she'd taken over his office. It was a nice office. It had almost been hers, until she'd been foolish enough to accept his offer. Lucilla pinched the bridge of her nose. Dammit.

She could still see him standing in front of the ossuary, still hear the trauma in his voice as he told her about his mother. If only she was as heartless as he was. If only she could have walked out of his house that morning and told him to hell with it, that she'd pay him his severance package and be glad of it.

But she hadn't. She'd stayed and she'd listened. Strangely, she was happy she had. Because she wasn't the sort of person who could ignore anyone's pain. Maybe that meant she wasn't as hard or cold as she needed to be, but she'd made her peace with that. If being ruthless meant she couldn't sleep at night, then she didn't want it.

She continued with the reports, then sent out some orders to the department heads and turned to look out at the park across the street. A smiling man and woman played with a toddler, and Lucilla's stomach ached with the knot of pain that had lodged inside it. Why did it hurt so much to watch others be happy? She was accustomed to it, wasn't she?

The door swung inward and she turned, ready to ask Jessie why she was barging in without knocking—Lucilla had learned that lesson, after all—but it wasn't Jessie standing in the doorway.

Lucilla's heart squeezed tight in her chest. Christos looked as handsome and remote as always, dressed in a pair of dark trousers and a crisp white shirt with gray pinstripes. His hair was mussed and his eyes were blood-shot. Her first instinct was to go to him, but she forced herself to remain seated as she let her gaze roll over him.

"We did not expect you back so soon," she said coolly, her heart thrumming an impossible rhythm. "In fact, I thought you were in Moscow today."

He raked a hand through his hair. "I was." He tossed his briefcase on a chair and stalked toward the desk. Lucilla swallowed hard. He stopped in front of her and she realized that he hadn't shaved this morning. Or, ap-parently, slept.

Lucilla got up, her heart lodging in her throat. "What's wrong, Christos? Has something happened?"

There had been no drama that she was aware of.

"I don't know," he said. He passed a hand over his face and then his eyes were hot on hers. "I miss you, Lucilla. That's not supposed to happen."

Myriad emotions washed over her then. Hope. Love. Anger. Fear. Despair.

"I don't know what that means, Christos. You're the one who decided we were finished."

"Perhaps I made a mistake."

Her pulse skipped. Tiny beads of sweat broke out on her skin. It was what she wanted, and yet…

It wasn't enough. This past week had been torture for her, knowing she'd been so bloody stupid as to fall for him when he wasn't very likely to fall in return. She knew what he was, what he did. Christos was a lover of women—many women. And she couldn't take just a piece of him when she wanted everything.

She deserved everything, damn him.

"What do you propose? That we take up where we left off? That I fall into your arms and be grateful for whatever scraps of affection you deign to give me?"

His brows drew together. "I did not say that."

"Then what are you saying?" She sounded shrill, and she did not like it. She modulated her tone. "Because I'm afraid I don't understand what you want."

He looked as if he were in pain. And then, just like that, he wiped away the look of uncertainty and became once more the cool, efficient Greek tycoon. "Isn't it obvious? I want you in my bed, Lucilla. I want more of what we had together in Greece."

"What did we have? Because I'm not sure."

He looked puzzled. "Sex. Heat. Companionship."

She was trembling. "I think you can get that anywhere. You don't need me for sex when you have a legion of women willing to provide it for you."

His jaw worked. "But I don't want them. I want you."

Lucilla's stomach went into free fall. It was what she wanted to hear. And yet…not. She swallowed against the sudden tightness in her throat. "Do you love me, Christos?"

He looked puzzled. And then he looked stunned, and her heart fell to the bottom of the chasm in her soul, where it shattered into a million shards of cut glass. *Well, what did you expect?*

"I am…fond of you." The words seemed to be dragged from him and she didn't know whether to be flattered or angered.

She came around the desk and stopped in front of him. She could feel his heat, smell his skin, and she wanted to melt into him the way she had countless times in Greece. But she had to be strong.

"Fond? I'm afraid that's not good enough." She tried not to get teary, but she could feel tears welling up behind her eyes. She lifted her hand to his jaw, smoothed it against his stubble-roughened skin. He turned his cheek into her palm and her heart throbbed painfully.

"I need more from you." She had to push the words past the tightness in her throat.

He looked wary. "More?"

She put her other palm on his cheek, cupped his face in her hands. "Yes, more." She sucked in a breath and plunged onward. "I can't be your temporary mistress. I can't be a hot office romance that's convenient for now. I can't be with you and wonder when it'll be over the next time, when you'll close yourself off from me and tell me you have to take a trip somewhere while I stay behind. I can't watch you arrive at a Chatsfield event with another woman on your arm. I won't do any of those things, Christos. So unless you can give me more, I think it's best we keep things the way they are."

His jaw worked. His eyes glittered. And then he tugged her against him and crushed his mouth down on hers. Her body dissolved as his beloved lips moved over hers. His tongue slid into her mouth and she moaned as she clung to him.

But that voice in the back of her head wouldn't let her enjoy the moment. It kept telling her she had to stand up for herself, that he was trying to kiss her into compliance without really giving her a thing. That he was imposing his will on her and trying to make her bend to it.

She pushed her palms against his chest—once, hard—and he let her go.

"Lucillitsa…" He swallowed. "I can't be what you want. I can't promise you anything. I can only be what I am, and I can only give you what is in my heart right this minute. I want you. I've tried not to, but I do. And that's more than I've given any woman."

She wrapped her arms around herself. "It's not enough." Her throat ached. Hadn't she been here before? In so many different ways than this one, she'd accepted less than she deserved because others claimed it was all they were capable of. "I'm tired of doing the best I can and it not being good enough. I'm tired of giving my all and having others give me a portion in return." She shook her head back and forth almost violently. "No, I won't do it. I won't accept it. It's all or nothing, Christos."

He stood there staring at her for so long, his eyes gleaming hot. And then he reached for his briefcase. "I have nothing to give you, Lucilla. Nothing."

Christos was bitterly angry. His life had always made sense to him, but now he couldn't find his equilibrium. He'd let Lucilla leave him in Greece. He'd watched her climb onto the helicopter, telling himself it was the right thing to let her go. She'd looked upset. There had been dark shadows under her eyes, hollows that he knew he'd put there, and he'd told himself it was best if he complied with her request to leave.

He'd intended to return to London with her, and then to begin his tour of the Chatsfield locations. But he couldn't make himself get on that helicopter, couldn't endure a long flight where he no longer had the right to touch her or kiss her or lose himself in her warmth.

The next day, rather than return to London, he'd begun his tour. And it had worked for the first few days.

He'd thrown himself into the job, evaluating the businesses and making much needed changes in New York and San Francisco. He'd congratulated himself on his ability to focus on work.

But the nights were hell. He kept thinking of Lucilla, kept imagining her there with him, her beautiful smile, her lush body, the sounds she made when she shattered, the way her body pulsed around him. He'd wanted her and he'd missed her, and that both stunned him and angered him.

Christos did not need anyone. He'd spent a lifetime not needing anyone. He'd learned, in the hell of his youth, that needing made you vulnerable. He couldn't go there ever again. It was too dangerous, too frightening.

It was so much easier not to love people. They couldn't disappoint you when you expected nothing from them. They couldn't hurt you when you didn't care.

He rubbed a hand over his chest, wondering why it ached when it wasn't supposed to. Lucilla was nothing special. She was a woman, like all women. Yes, he was intrigued by her. Yes, he wanted her still. He wanted her beneath him, wanted her voice in his ear, his name on her lips.

But how was he supposed to have these things when she wouldn't comply? When she demanded he give her things he would give to no one? Things he no longer possessed?

He didn't have a heart, dammit. He'd carved it out in juvenile detention, and he'd kept the space where it was supposed to be empty as he'd moved through his life, ruthlessly slashing and burning everything in his path.

He was precisely what he'd wanted to be. Successful,

rich, emotionless, unattached to anyone or anything. It was safe.

He let himself into his apartment and dropped his briefcase on the floor. It was quiet, empty, and for the first time he could ever remember, he didn't like the emptiness. Maybe he would get a cat. Not a dog, because dogs needed to be walked, but a cat, a creature wary and remote like himself.

Christos swore as he went over to the liquor cabinet and poured a finger of Scotch into a tumbler. He was thinking of cats now? Of acquiring one and spending his nights cooped up with the creature in this apartment? Had it really come to this?

He stalked through the apartment and into the library where an easel stood draped in cloth. He stared at the cloth, wondering why he'd bought the damn thing beneath it and if he dared to look at it.

Furious with himself, he whipped the cloth away from the painting. A woman laughed at him from the canvas. A woman who looked very much like the one he'd left standing in his office at the Chatsfield.

She was lovely, but not as lovely as Lucilla. He looked at the way her head tilted, at the way the artist had painted her laughter. She seemed happy, yet she'd harbored so much unhappiness that she'd abandoned her family twenty years ago and never returned. He understood that kind of unhappiness.

Christos tossed the liquor back and it scalded his throat as it burned a path into his belly. He turned away from the portrait and stalked out of the library. He'd learned a long time ago that the only way to deal with pain was to confront it head-on. And then to obliterate it.

* * *

Lucilla did not see Christos for the next several days. He returned to the office, but she avoided him completely. She didn't even make the morning staff meetings. And Christos did not summon her. He sent her emails. She replied to the ones she had to reply to and let Jessie answer the rest. Jessie had been handling everything well enough in Sophie's absence that Christos insisted he didn't need another assistant just yet.

Christos rescheduled the shareholders' meeting and Lucilla accepted it on her tablet's calendar, already thinking of possible excuses to miss it. But she knew she could not. It was the one meeting where she had to face him and she would do so with steel in her spine.

But, oh, how she missed him. She was so furious with herself, and furious with him. He'd told her he missed her, but he clearly did not miss her enough. She was replaceable in his life and she kept waiting for the moment when he would appear in the tabloids with another woman on his arm. It was inevitable and she told herself she would survive it.

Though she'd been looking at vacation packages just in case. She had brochures for Mallorca, Hawaii, Tenerife, Saint Kitts. Any of them would do in a crisis, though Hawaii was the most remote and perhaps the best fit because of it. She fingered the brochure again, stroked the glossy photo of a palm tree at sunset and a woman in a grass skirt. Paradise. Peace.

If only it were that easy.

The morning of the shareholders' meeting dawned and Lucilla dressed carefully in a tailored suit the color of eggplant. She put on a pair of tall nude heels, swiped on fresh lipstick and started to wind her hair into a bun.

But as she looked at herself in the mirror, she made the decision to leave it down. Christos liked it down. Not that she was doing it to please him. No, she was doing it because she wanted to. Because she liked the way the color looked against her suit jacket and because it made her feel pretty.

Then she squared her jaw, grabbed her purse and briefcase and headed for the office.

The meeting was being held in one of the main ballrooms of the hotel and it was packed with attendees. Lucilla walked in with her head held high and took her seat in the front row. Christos stood on the platform that had been set up for the purpose, his head bowed as he went over his notes. Her heart skipped a beat as she watched him. The light shone down on his glossy black head, picked out the lines of his handsome face. He wore a tie today. She imagined loosening it, tugging it free, and closed her eyes as pain washed over her.

She would never be that close to him again. She couldn't bear the thought that she wouldn't, but what choice did she have? She would not live half a life with him, always waiting for their affair to end. She couldn't.

"Good morning, everyone," Christos finally said when the ballroom was packed. "Welcome to the annual general meeting of the Chatsfield Group. There are the usual reports to go over, naturally, and then you must vote for your board of directors, the same as every year. You have the candidates' bios before you." People riffled through the papers in the folders they'd been given. "As you are aware, the board of directors appoints the chief executive. I therefore must make an announcement before we continue."

Lucilla's heart began to thrum hard. And then Christos's head came up and his eyes met hers across the sea of people. It was as if they were alone in the room together and she wanted more than anything to tell him not to say another word, not to do whatever it was that he was about to do. She didn't know what he would say, but she shot to her feet as if doing so could prevent him from speaking.

"Today, I offer you my resignation," Christos said, his gaze still holding hers. "And I submit to you that Lucilla Chatsfield should now be your CEO."

CHAPTER FOURTEEN

THE BALLROOM ERUPTED. It was no murmur that swept over the crowd. It was a rush of sound, like a wildfire, and it spread to all corners of the room simultaneously. Christos was only aware of Lucilla. She stood in that sea of people as they tugged on her sleeves and pelted her with questions, but she didn't take her gaze from his.

Her eyes, those lovely brown eyes with the golden flecks, were wide and wounded. He knew it even from here. It was hot in the spotlight but he didn't shrink from its glare. There were reporters in the room—there were always reporters at the annual meetings—and they were frantically writing in their notebooks and on their tablets. A few tried to get to Lucilla, who was not at all prepared for the onslaught, and that was the moment when Christos knew he had to get this meeting back on track.

By the end, she would have accustomed herself to the idea and she would know what to say to the reporters. But first they had to get through the meeting.

Christos raised his voice, thundered into the microphone and asked everyone to sit. It took a few moments, but the room grew silent again. Lucilla had sunk into her chair, but her eyes hadn't left his face. As much as he wanted to only look at her, he had a job to do.

"There is much business to be done this morning," he said tightly. "There will be time for questions after."

He began the process of conducting the meeting but his mind was only partly on what he was doing. The rest was on Lucilla. He'd realized in the past week that zhe could no longer stay in London. He couldn't work in the same building and not want her. He couldn't live in the same city and not ache for her. He didn't know what the hell this was, but he had to break away from it.

And he had to give her back the inheritance that was rightfully hers. She was capable of running the Chatsfield empire, of overseeing the vast holdings and making the right decisions for the company. She was the one Chatsfield he believed in. The one he trusted. And he would no longer stand in her way.

She wanted him gone. If he gave her nothing else, he would give her that. It was the least he could do for her.

When the AGM was over, he exited the ballroom by a rear door and wound his way through the offices until he could emerge onto the street and into the waiting limo. The driver sped away just as a crowd boiled out the doors to the Chatsfield HQ.

His phone started to ring in earnest and he glanced at the display. He recognized the company name but rather than take the call he shut the phone off. He knew this game. Someone had heard he'd resigned from the Chatsfield and wanted to snag him before another company did. His phone would ring incessantly as the offers poured in. He did not want to field them today.

The limo dropped him at his loft apartment and he went inside, debating whether to stay in London a few more days or hop on his plane tonight. He could go wherever he wanted, but he was unaccustomed to having nothing to do. He'd been working since the day he'd left the juvenile-detention facility. Always in the past when he'd left a job, it was for a better job.

He'd never quit because of a woman before. He stopped in the middle of his living room and blinked as the import of what he'd done hit him. He'd made the decision earlier in the week. He'd drank himself into a stupor—very unlike him—and then, in the middle of the night when he'd been at least half-sober, he'd called a cab and ridden to her apartment. He'd stood in the street beneath her building, staring up at her window, and wondered what in the hell he was doing.

She tangled him up inside. Made him feel things he wasn't supposed to feel. Made him want more than he knew was safe. He'd wanted, desperately, to go up to her apartment and take her in his arms.

And because he'd wanted it desperately, he'd climbed back inside the cab and gone home. Now, he went into his bedroom and took a suitcase from the closet. He was accustomed to leaving everything behind and moving on. Today was no different. He would take his time, pick a new company to rescue and have his things sent when he was ready for them.

He finished packing the suitcase, rang for a car and then went into the library and stopped in front of the painting. He had not covered it back up. He'd forced himself to live with it, day in and day out, as if he could inoculate himself to the pain by doing so.

But he was finished with it now, like he was finished with everything here. He would have it wrapped up and sent over to Lucilla. Anonymously, of course. She need never know that he had purchased it that night. He still didn't know why he'd done so, or what he'd thought he might do with the painting once he had, but she'd been so sad and affected that he'd known he couldn't let it go to someone else.

He'd never quite planned beyond the moment, but he'd never intended to keep it, either.

He heard the elevator open and he turned, annoyed that the doorman had let the driver come up. He did not need help to carry his bags. But when he walked back into the living area, it wasn't a uniformed chauffeur standing there.

Lucilla looked furious. And so beautiful she made his heart contract into a tight knot in his chest.

"You coward," she grated. "You bloody, stupid ass. What were you thinking?"

Lucilla's entire being trembled with fury and fear and hurt. Christos stood across the room from her, his body tall and erect, his handsome face as remote as ever. She wanted to throw herself at him and claw his eyes out. And she wanted to sink to the floor and ask him why. Why couldn't he love her? Why was he so determined to ruin everything he'd begun by pulling that stunt at the AGM?

He arched a cool eyebrow. "I believe I was giving you what you have always claimed to want. My absence."

She stalked toward him. And then she stopped before she got too close, before she lost control of her emotions simply from proximity to him. "You could have asked me what *I* wanted."

He looked surprised. "Ask you? You have made it clear from the beginning what you wanted. I did not imagine that had changed simply because I forced you to come to Greece with me."

She'd been asking herself for the past two hours, since he'd made that announcement, just why she was so upset with him for it. Because she *had* wanted to be the chief executive. Because she believed she was the right person for the job. She'd wanted it so much she could taste it, but when he'd handed it to her on a platter, she found she didn't like the taste all that well, after all.

"I thought we had something in Greece," she said, and then cursed herself for sounding so sad and needy.

He swallowed, and her heart skipped a beat at that little chink in his armor. Maybe she was too hopeful, but she couldn't help it.

"We did."

A wave of feeling washed over her, bathing her in heat and despair. "Then why, Christos? Why did you push me away? And why are you leaving?"

He shoved both hands through his hair and then shook his head softly. "I don't know how to do this, Lucillitsa."

She took a halting step toward him. "How to do what?"

His gaze speared into her, his icy blue eyes hot with emotions she'd never seen there before. He seemed on the edge of his control, and it gave her a perverse kind of hope that she didn't dare to believe was real.

"I don't know how to be with you. How to...*love* you."

The lump in her throat swelled. Her eyes blurred. "I believe you do."

He was shaking his head. "It's better if I go. Better for both of us."

Lucilla stiffened her spine and glared at him through her tears. "Until today, I've never thought you a coward, Christos. But you are. You can't face the truly difficult tasks. You told me I couldn't make the hard decisions, but it's *you* who cannot make them. You who would run away when you should stay, you who would give up—"

Here, her voice choked off. She tried to finish the sentence, but her vocal chords refused to obey. Christos didn't say a word.

She backed away from him, turned to go. It was useless. He was determined not to feel anything for anyone, and she couldn't force him to do so.

Strong arms wrapped around her, pulled her backward until she was wedged tightly to his body. She hadn't heard him move, but she slumped against him, giving in to the pleasure of his embrace. Even if it was the last time. Even if it was nothing more than this simple touch.

"Lucilla." His breath ruffled her hair, and then his mouth was at her ear. "I am damaged, Lucilla *mou*. Broken. I don't know how to give you what you want. I wish I did, but I would only hurt you in the end."

She shuddered in his arms as his warm breath washed over her skin. She wanted to turn, wanted to kiss him, wanted to make him realize the truth of this thing between them. But he wouldn't let her. So she settled for the only weapon she had.

"I love you, Christos. I love you."

His grip on her tightened. And then it fell away, as she knew it must. She took advantage of it to turn, to cup both his cheeks in her palms.

"Allow me to make my own choices, Christos. You told me I wasn't willing to make hard choices, but I am. And if loving you is a hard choice, then I'm making it." A tear spilled free to slide down her cheek. "You can't stop me from loving you. You can leave and you can pretend like it never happened, but you can't stop me. I will love you no matter where you go."

He shuddered beneath her touch, his long eyelashes dipping down to cover his eyes. She had no idea what he was thinking, no idea what was about to happen. But she couldn't let him go without telling him how she felt. She'd always played things safely, always tried to take care of everyone else but herself. Well, maybe this wasn't quite taking care of herself, but at least she would know she'd done everything she could. She would not second-guess herself once he was gone.

"I don't know if I can love you," he said softly. "I don't know if I can love anyone."

She had to hold back the anguished cry that begged for escape. "You can, Christos." She said it firmly. "I heard it in your voice in the cemetery. I saw it in your eyes. You loved someone and you lost her, but that doesn't make you dead inside."

His eyes were a brilliant blue. "I feel dead inside, *agapi mou*. I always have."

She sucked in a breath. "Always? Every moment of every day? Every minute we spent together?"

He swallowed. "No. Not every moment."

She gave him a watery smile. "See? Progress."

He took her wrists in his hands and pulled her palms from his face. Then he kissed them both and let her go. "That's not good enough. Not for you. You're a good woman, Lucilla. You deserve a good man."

"There you go again," she said softly, past the lump in her throat. "Making assumptions and giving orders. I'll decide who's good enough for me, thank you."

He checked his watch. "The car will be here by now." He went and grabbed his suitcase and her heart throbbed hot and fast. He stopped at the elevator and turned back to her. "There's something for you in the library. I was going to have it sent to you, but you can make those arrangements now."

Her legs trembled as she watched him step onto the elevator. "If you walk away, I won't wait for you forever," she said, her voice thick with pain. "I'll move on. I'll find someone else to love and I'll forget all about you."

She never would forget him, but she was angry and hurt and she had to lash out or explode. Christos only smiled sadly.

"I hope you do, Lucilla *mou*. I pray you do."

The limo was nearly to the airport when Christos suddenly couldn't breathe. He put a hand over his chest and worked on pulling air in and out of his lungs, methodically, while a sensation very much like panic crawled down his spine and back up again. He'd felt this way before, long ago, when he'd been a kid trying to escape his father's wrath and then later when he'd found himself in juvenile detention and responsible for his own survival in that horrible place.

If he hadn't known it was a panic attack, he would have made the driver take him straight to the hospital as his chest squeezed tight and sweat broke out on his skin. He closed his eyes and leaned his head back against the seat. It was panic, nothing more than panic.

It would pass.

And yet all he could see when he closed his eyes was Lucilla. Her face had been so wounded when he'd stepped into that elevator. She'd told him she wouldn't wait, that she would find someone else to love—

His chest squeezed tighter than before and he wondered if he really were having a heart attack. But then the pain eased when he thought of Lucilla's hands on his face, of her sweet voice telling him she loved him. *She loved him.*

That thought made warmth spread through his chest and his breathing eased. But then the driver took the exit for Heathrow and the tightness started again. Christos looked out the window at the traffic, at the planes crowding the sky, and he suddenly wanted to howl. He imagined himself getting on board the jet, strapping into his seat and leaning his head back after he told the pilot to take him…where? He had no idea where he was going yet, no idea where he wanted to be.

Not true.

He did know where he wanted to be. He wanted to be in Lucilla's arms. In her bed. He'd wanted that for weeks now, and he'd had it for a brief while. But he had to do the right thing and let her go. He had to get out of her life and let her run her company, let her find a man who would love her as she deserved.

The thought of Lucilla with another man tightened the bands around his chest again. He tried to picture it, tried to force himself through the pain so he could make it to the other side. But everything within him rebelled. One word echoed through his brain: *mine.*

He wanted Lucilla. He wanted her in his life and he wanted to try and be what she needed him to be. Christos blinked as another feeling began to swell inside him. It was as if he'd fought so long and so hard and then let down his guard, just for a moment, and the enemy at the gates had broken through.

Except it wasn't an enemy at all. It was salvation.

Fear and hope washed over him at once. His voice burst forth in a roar that came from the very depths of his soul. "We have to go back!"

* * *

Lucilla didn't have the strength to leave Christos's apartment just yet. She found the library and gaped at the painting sitting there. Her mother looked so happy and beautiful in the portrait. Lucilla wished, just for a moment, that her mother was here, that she could ask for advice. That she could sit at her mother's feet, lay her head on her mother's lap and cry. Just for once, couldn't she put the burden of her feelings onto someone else?

She sank down on the carpet and sat there, staring up at the painting, feeling bitter and angry at the world. She'd never had anyone to rely on, never been able to lean on another soul except herself. She'd spent her life making sure everyone else was okay, trying to make her father proud of her—and yes, trying to be so good in the hopes her mother would come home again—and what did she have to show for it?

Nothing. Oh, she had what she thought she'd always wanted—leadership of the company—but it was an empty victory. What a fool she'd been.

Lucilla wiped her fingers beneath her eyes as the tears kept coming and dried them on her skirt. God, she was pitiful. She wanted someone to lean on, just once in a while, but she'd learned again and again that there was no one. There was only her.

Christos didn't want her. Her own mother didn't want her. Her father was off in America with his new fiancé, and all her siblings had their own lives. She was as alone as she'd ever been.

And she was angry, dammit. She curled her hands into fists and sat there on the floor until the dam burst. Then she was crying and beating her fists against the carpet, screaming and ranting and hurting. Vaguely, she knew she was a mess. A histrionic, dramatic mess. An embarrassment.

But she couldn't stop. She sobbed until she had no tears left and then she surged up off the floor and knocked the portrait off the easel. It bounced onto the carpet with a great whack and then fell onto its face.

Lucilla gritted her teeth together and sucked in deep breaths. She wanted to stomp a hole in the damn thing and she wanted to grab it up and hug it close and tell her mother she was sorry.

"Lucillitsa."

She spun around to find Christos standing in the doorway. "Damn you," she growled, her heart breaking anew at the sight of him. He'd no doubt forgotten his passport or something equally trivial and had returned for it only to find her still here, making a mess of his pristine dwelling.

"I'm sorry."

"Sorry?" She clenched her fists at her sides. She knew she looked like hell, but what did it matter now? "That's not a good enough word to atone for what you've done to me. I wish you'd never come to the Chatsfield, and I damn sure wish I'd never stayed in Greece with you."

"Agapi mou."

She closed her eyes tight. She had to cling to her anger to stay sane. "What did I tell you about calling me pet names, Christos? And what does this one mean, anyway? My little snowflake or something?"

"It means 'my love.'"

She didn't think her heart could hurt any worse. She was wrong. Fresh tears welled behind her eyes. "That's not funny."

"It's not meant to be."

She opened her eyes again and met his brilliant blue gaze. "I was just going. Get your passport or whatever you forgot and don't worry about me."

"Lucillitsa." He came over and took her hand in his. She tried to snatch it away but he was too strong. He put her hand on his chest, tugged her closer. "Feel this. Feel what you do to me."

She shook her head, too afraid to let even a kernel of hope take root once more. "I don't know what you're getting at. I'm tired and angry and I just want to go home. I can't do this again. I can't."

He slid his other hand along her jaw, speared his fingers into her hair. "My heart, Lucilla. Feel my heart." He pressed her hand harder against his chest and she felt the roar of his blood. "It's racing because I'm terrified."

"I don't underst—"

He cut her off. "Tell me I'm not too late. Tell me I haven't lost you."

She was utterly and completely numb. And then a tiny bud of happiness began to grow in her belly, spreading and unfurling and warming her cold, cold veins. Maybe she should be more cautious, but she was too spent to care. "You haven't lost me, Christos. Not in the space of an hour. Not even in the space of weeks, when I should have stopped loving you utterly if I could have."

He dragged her into his arms and held her tightly. Her ear was to his chest and she marveled at the reckless beat of his heart. For a moment, she thought she must be dreaming. She'd fallen asleep on the carpet in his library and she was dreaming that he'd returned, that he wanted her. It was the only logical explanation.

But then she dug her fingernails into her palms and

felt the bite of pain and she knew she wasn't asleep. Still, she pushed back until she could look up into Christos's eyes. She was awake, but that explained nothing.

"I still don't understand what's happened. You left. You said you couldn't love me. So why are you back?"

He dragged in a breath. "Because you were right, *agapi mou*. Because I am a coward and a fool and an ass, and it was easier to walk out than to stay. I've always walked away when things got too difficult. I've spent a lifetime not getting attached to anyone, to pulling up stakes and moving on to the next challenge. I thought that was the hard part—leaving and starting again—but it's not. The hard part is staying."

She was clutching his shirt in her fists. "I believe you can do anything you set your mind to, Christos. You remade yourself into a man who is brilliant, honorable and successful. Your mother would be proud of you."

His smile was both sad and tender. "I think she would, but I also think she would have been angry with me for walking out on you earlier. She would have known what I did not."

Her pulse skipped and slid recklessly. Was this really happening? "And what is that?"

"That you are part of me. That I've wanted you from the first moment I saw you. That you are the one woman in this world I was meant to love."

"You're going to make me cry."

He kissed her softly. "I don't want to make you cry. I want to make you happy."

"I am happy. And scared. I need you too much, Christos, and it worries me."

"I understand this more than you know. I thought I

was having a heart attack when I reached Heathrow. But it was simply my heart breaking because I'd left you."

She didn't want to ask the question, but she had to know the answer. It was all or nothing, no matter how good it felt to be in his arms again. "Does this mean you love me?"

He closed his eyes for a moment, as if he were gathering his courage. "Yes. So much it terrifies me. You are the strongest, bravest, most beautiful woman I know. And I *am* the man you deserve, because there is no other who will ever love you like I do."

Lucilla's knees went weak. And then she laughed. "That's the Christos I know and love. So certain of himself. So arrogant and bossy."

He speared his fingers into her hair and sifted the heavy strands. "It turns you on when I'm bossy. It always has."

"Yes, I'll admit that now. I like it when you tell me what to do. It gives me great pleasure to do the opposite."

He laughed. "Then don't kiss me, Lucilla. Don't touch me or tell me you love me. Never do that."

"It's a deal," she said, spreading her hands over the contours of his chest. "I love you, Christos. So much."

And then she kissed him.

EPILOGUE

Several months later...

THE WEDDING OF Gene Chatsfield to Helena Morgan was the talk of the society pages. The reception was held at the flagship Chatsfield Hotel in London, where all the Chatsfield children returned to celebrate with their father and the woman he adored. It was nearly Christmas now, and the hotel was decorated to celebrate the season. Even with Christmas trees, lights and garland, there was no doubt it was a celebration of marriage taking place today and not a Christmas party.

The bride was lovely in a cream gown, and Lucilla's father was handsome in his tuxedo. He clearly doted on his new bride, and Lucilla was happy for him. They'd had a talk earlier and he'd told her how proud he was of her and the job she'd been doing. She'd been stunned, and then she'd been pleased. She'd ceased needing her father's approval but it had still been nice to hear it.

Lucilla stopped at the bar to speak with the reception manager. The toast was coming soon and she wanted to make sure they had plenty of Rubida, a lovely sparkling wine that came from their exclusive new supplier, Purman Wines of Australia. Franco had done an outstanding job of convincing Purman Wines to sign with them. Not only that, but he'd also convinced Miss Holly Purman to wear his engagement ring. He looked blissfully happy where he stood with his fiancée, and Lucilla smiled to herself.

Across the room, she caught Antonio's eye. He was with his new wife, Orla, and he finally seemed settled in a way she hadn't thought he ever would be. Her heart filled with happiness at the look in his eyes when he turned to smile at his wife again.

Lucilla continued across the room, letting her gaze slide over the gathering as she picked out the rest of her baby chicks.

Nicolo sat at a table with Sophie, his pregnant bride and Christos's former PA. Lucilla chuckled to herself when she thought back to the utter shock with which Christos had greeted the resignation of his PA and the reason for it. He'd taken it in stride, however, and hired another PA—a man this time, which Lucilla found amusing. She'd assured him she did not care if he hired a beauty queen, so long as the woman could do the job. She believed in Christos's love and commitment to her.

At the same table sat Orsino and Poppy, who held hands and looked utterly in love as they chatted with Lucca and Charlotte. And then there was Aaliyah, their newest sibling, a half sister whom their father had introduced to them all only recently. She was dark and lovely as she sat with her husband, Sheikh Sayed, the heir to the throne of Zeena Sahra. She'd seemed very shy when she'd been introduced to them all, but Lucilla had discovered that she was actually quite strong when one got to know her. It had been a bit of a shock to discover they had a half sibling they knew nothing of, but

Lucilla did what came natural to her: she took the newest chick under her metaphorical wing and added her to the list of people she cared about.

Finally, there was Cara, who stood with their father and his new wife. And Cara's new husband, Aiden. Lucilla loved all her siblings, but Cara held the most special place in her heart. Seeing her darling baby girl settled and happy eased Lucilla's mind about her youngest sister. Perhaps Lucilla had done a good job, after all.

"You're thinking too much," Christos said, sliding up behind her where she'd stopped in a doorway and turned to look back at everyone. His hands came around her waist, settled on her hips as he held her firmly to him.

His breath feathered over her skin and she shivered. "I'm thinking how wonderful this day has turned out. And how happy everyone is."

Christos nuzzled her ear. She thought perhaps she should tell him to be discreet, but she found she didn't actually care. "I'm happy," he said. "Blissfully happy."

"So am I. Especially after that thing you did this morning."

Christos chuckled. "I would love to do it again. How about we disappear into your office for a bit?"

"Naughty man. I meant later."

"If you can wait that long."

"Tease."

He pulled her harder against him, until she felt the evidence of his arousal against her bottom. Lucilla gasped.

"Who's the tease?" he growled in her ear.

Her body liquefied. "Christos, you make me want to do the most shocking things."

"God, I hope so."

Lucilla swallowed. "I don't know how I can wait. But

I have to. There's the toast, and then the dancing and who knows what else…."

He turned her in his arms until she was facing him. "There's something we need to discuss, Lucilla."

She smoothed her hands over his tuxedo jacket. Dear heaven, he was a handsome man. And he was *hers*.

"What is that, darling? Has your consultancy fee gone up again? You know I'll pay it. The Chatsfield needs your expertise—"

He put a finger over her lips. "No. I'm exclusively yours, my love. No other hotels may have my advice so long as you're in charge of the Chatsfield." He took his finger away from her lips and she trembled at the look in his eyes. Oh, he made her want to shimmy out of her gown right here and now. His gaze lifted, scanned the crowd behind her. "All this wedding fever. It's contagious, Lucilla."

Her heart began to hammer at the look in his eyes.

"I was going to wait until later to say this, but I can't. I want you to marry me. Waking up in your arms is no longer enough for me. I want to know you won't leave me, that no other man will ever have a claim on you. I want to see you grow big with our child and I want to hold your hand on the beach in Greece when we are so old our kids have to push us out there in our wheelchairs."

Her eyes were filling with tears. Dammit, it was too soon to be hormonal. Or maybe not. "That's the most beautiful thing you've ever said to me."

He swallowed and for a moment she saw the scared little boy lurking behind the eyes of the enigmatic man. "I want to say beautiful things to you always."

She leaned up and kissed him, her heart so full she

thought it would burst. "Yes, Christos. I will marry you."
She took his hand and brought it down to her belly,
pressed it against her. "And it's a good thing you asked.
I'll be growing big sooner than you might imagine."

He looked stunned as he processed that bit of information. And then he closed his eyes and tilted his head
back. The words he spoke were Greek, but she didn't
need to know what they were to know he was pleased.
She'd only found out a couple of days ago and she'd
been planning to tell him as soon as the chaos of the
wedding and reception were over. They were flying to
Kefalonia for Christmas in a few days and she'd wanted
to tell him there.

But this was so much better. As long as she lived, she
would never forget the look on his face. The utter joy
and the love for her—and their baby—shining through.

"I love you, Lucilla. I don't know how I made it
through life without you. Until you came along, I thought
I had a good life. I had no idea how wrong I was."

Happiness swelled inside her, fluttered in her chest
like a baby bird. "I think it will only get better from
here."

He brought her hand up to his mouth and kissed it
reverently. "And I *know* it will."

* * * * *

If you loved THE CHATSFIELDS,
the story will continue in 2015!

COMING NEXT MONTH FROM

HARLEQUIN Presents®

Available December 16, 2014

#3297 SHEIKH'S DESERT DUTY
The Chatsfield
by Maisey Yates

Sheikh Zayn Al-Ahmar must stop journalist Sophie from destroying his world—so he kidnaps her! But soon Sophie's delectable company puts everything he values at risk. Only one mistress can rule Zayn's heart—will it be Sophie, or his duty?

#3298 THE SECRET HIS MISTRESS CARRIED
by Lynne Graham

Billie fought hard to heal her broken heart after Gio Letsos married someone else. When he storms back into her life, she's determined not to fall for his seduction again. Especially because she has a secret to protect...their son.

#3299 NINE MONTHS TO REDEEM HIM
by Jennie Lucas

I gave Edward St. Cyr my body, which he wanted, and my heart, which he didn't. Did I make a major mistake? Maybe when he knows about our baby it will heal his heart so he can love us both...

#3300 TO SIN WITH THE TYCOON
Seven Sexy Sins
by Cathy Williams

Gabriel Cabrera can get *anything* he wants...until he meets PA Alice Morgan. So he'll draw her to him, his every touch sinfully seductive. And sweet, virginal Alice will come to him willingly so Gabriel can claim his prize...

#3301 FONSECA'S FURY
Billionaire Brothers
by Abby Green

The last time Luca Fonseca saw Serena DePiero, he'd ended up in a jail cell. So when he discovers she's working for *his* charity, his anger reignites. Serena can handle anything...except the passion that flares hotter than Luca's fury.

#3302 INHERITED BY HER ENEMY
by Sara Craven

As the final words of Virginia Mason's stepfather's will are read, her innocent life suddenly shatters. With no inheritance, her future—and her family's—is entirely in the hands of enigmatic and outrageously attractive Frenchman Andre Duchard.

#3303 THE RUSSIAN'S ULTIMATUM
by Michelle Smart

Emily Richardson has Pascha Virshilas's private documents to blackmail him into clearing her father's name...but Pascha has his own terms. Emily must accompany him to his private island, where the wind blows aside suspicions to reveal something much more dangerous—lust!

#3304 THE LAST HEIR OF MONTERRATO
by Andie Brock

Rafael Revaldi needs an heir, but first he must win back his estranged wife! Lottie returns to the castle she once called home, but can she risk her heart again to give them the child they both so desperately want?

REQUEST YOUR FREE BOOKS!

HARLEQUIN *Presents*

2 FREE NOVELS PLUS
2 FREE GIFTS!

PASSION
GUARANTEED
SEDUCTION

YES! Please send me 2 FREE Harlequin Presents® novels and my 2 FREE gifts (gifts are worth about $10). After receiving them, if I don't wish to receive any more books, I can return the shipping statement marked "cancel." If I don't cancel, I will receive 6 brand-new novels every month and be billed just $4.30 per book in the U.S. or $4.99 per book in Canada. That's a saving of at least 14% off the cover price! It's quite a bargain! Shipping and handling is just 50¢ per book in the U.S. and 75¢ per book in Canada.* I understand that accepting the 2 free books and gifts places me under no obligation to buy anything. I can always return a shipment and cancel at any time. Even if I never buy another book, the two free books and gifts are mine to keep forever.

106/306 HDN FVRK

Name _____
(PLEASE PRINT)

Address _____ Apt. #

City _____ State/Prov. _____ Zip/Postal Code

Signature (if under 18, a parent or guardian must sign)

Mail to the **Harlequin® Reader Service:**
IN U.S.A.: P.O. Box 1867, Buffalo, NY 14240-1867
IN CANADA: P.O. Box 609, Fort Erie, Ontario L2A 5X3

**Are you a current subscriber to Harlequin Presents books
and want to receive the larger-print edition?
Call 1-800-873-8635 or visit www.ReaderService.com.**

* Terms and prices subject to change without notice. Prices do not include applicable taxes. Sales tax applicable in N.Y. Canadian residents will be charged applicable taxes. Offer not valid in Quebec. This offer is limited to one order per household. Not valid for current subscribers to Harlequin Presents books. All orders subject to credit approval. Credit or debit balances in a customer's account(s) may be offset by any other outstanding balance owed by or to the customer. Please allow 4 to 6 weeks for delivery. Offer available while quantities last.

Your Privacy—The Harlequin® Reader Service is committed to protecting your privacy. Our Privacy Policy is available online at www.ReaderService.com or upon request from the Harlequin Reader Service.

We make a portion of our mailing list available to reputable third parties that offer products we believe may interest you. If you prefer that we not exchange your name with third parties, or if you wish to clarify or modify your communication preferences, please visit us at www.ReaderService.com/consumerschoice or write to us at Harlequin Reader Service Preference Service, P.O. Box 9062, Buffalo, NY 14269. Include your complete name and address.

* * *

RESTIVE as a cat on hot bricks, Billie peered out of the
window as Gio sprang out of the limo, and she tensed
up even more at the sight of his formal attire. He wore
a faultlessly tailored black business suit teamed with a
white shirt and purple tie. This was Gio in full tycoon
mode, eyes veiled, lean, strong face taut with reserve, and
unsmiling.

"I have something to tell you," she said breathlessly in
the hall.

Gio withdrew a folded sheet of paper from his jacket and
simply extended it. "I already know…"

Her heart beating very fast, Billie shook open the sheet,
lashes fluttering in disconcertment when she saw the
photocopy of the birth certificate. "I don't know what to
say—"

"There's nothing you can say," Gio pronounced icily.
"You lied last night. You deliberately concealed the truth
from me for well over a year. Evidently you had no intention
of *ever* telling me that I was a father."

"I never expected to see you again," Billie muttered weakly.

"I want to see him," Gio breathed in a driven undertone.

"He's having a nap—"

Poised at the foot of the stairs, Gio gave her a sardonic appraisal. "I will still see him…"

Billie breathed in deep and started up the stairs, brushing damp palms down over her jeans. If she was reasonable, even a touch conciliating, they could deal with this situation in a perfectly civilized fashion, she told herself soothingly. Naturally Gio's first reaction was curiosity and, since he was now divorced, Theo's existence was probably less of an embarrassment than it might otherwise have been.

Billie pressed open the door. Theo's cot was in the corner. Gio strode up to the rails and gazed down with a powerful sense of disbelief at the baby peacefully sleeping in a tangle of covers. *His son*. Even at first glance, the family resemblance was staggering. Theo had a shock of black curls, a strong little nose and the set of his eyes was the same as Gio's. Gio breathed in deep and slow, his broad chest tightening on a surge of emotion unlike anything he had ever felt.

* * *

Will Gio forgive Billie for withholding the truth…
and admit his feelings for her?
Find out in
THE SECRET HIS MISTRESS CARRIED
January 2015

www.Harlequin.com